COKE BOYS

Romell Tukes

Lock Down Publications and Ca$h
Presents
Coke Boys
A Novel by *Romell Tukes*

Romell Tukes

Lock Down Publications
Po Box 944
Stockbridge, Ga 30281

Visit our website @
www.lockdownpublications.com

Copyright 2022 by Romell Tukes
Coke Boys

Lock Down Publications
Like our page on Facebook: Lock Down Publications @
www.facebook.com/lockdownpublications.ldp
Book interior design by: **Shawn Walker**

Stay Connected with Us!

Text **LOCKDOWN** to 22828 to stay up-to-date with new releases,
sneak peaks, contests and more…
Thank you.

Submission Guideline.

Submit the first three chapters of your completed manuscript to ldpsubmissions@gmail.com, subject line: Your book's title. The manuscript must be in a .doc file and sent as an attachment. Document should be in Times New Roman, double spaced and in size 12 font. Also, provide your synopsis and full contact information. If sending multiple submissions, they must each be in a separate email.

Have a story but no way to send it electronically? You can still submit to LDP/Ca$h Presents. Send in the first three chapters, written or typed, of your completed manuscript to:

LDP: Submissions Dept
Po Box 944
Stockbridge, Ga 30281

DO NOT send original manuscript. Must be a duplicate.

Provide your synopsis and a cover letter containing your full contact information.

Thanks for considering LDP and Ca$h Presents.

Acknowledgements

First, all praises are due to Allah. Shout to the readers and supporters, y'all know da vibes. We litty. You finna enjoy this movie. Shout Yonkers, NY CB, Frazier, YB, SG, Lingo, Brisco, Red, Fresh, Baby James, Banger, Chino, and Morano. Shout Spice from Newbury. Shout Dex from S. I., shout my BK fam OG Chuck, Tails, Tim Doby, Gunny and G59 niggas and the Woo's. Shout to my BX niggas Melly, Hump, DMU from Burnside, Juice Da Ape, and Spazz from Brooklyn, Zikka, and Hollywood. Shout to my N.C. guys from Bull City to Da Faye and Greensboro. Shout my Philly brothers Muchie, Big C, Dame, and Laz. Free da real rights locked up. Shout to LDP and Ca$h and once again big love to all the readers. I am the HOV of the pen game and this ink don't dry, big facts. Your talent is only good when you believe in yourself.

Romell Tukes

Chapter 1
Raleigh, N.C.

"This the same shit as last time?" Chubs stood over the twenty keys of uncut coke.

"Nigga, I would've told you if it wasn't," Hustle said, looking around the parking lot to see if the coast was still clear while they did the business transaction.

"I'm just asking," Chubs said, pulling out a bag of money.

"So you fucking with me from here on out?" Hustle asked.

Hustle was one of the biggest dope boys in Raleigh, besides a few other dope pushers.

"Yeah, this shit pure. Will be having too much cut in his shit sometimes," Chubs said, laughing.

"That's your man, bruh." Hustle opened the bag of money to make sure it looked like a reasonable amount.

"Fuck him. That nigga fucked my ex-bitch," Chubs said upset.

"So, this your get back?" Hustle handed him the drugs.

"Yeah, but what's your real beef with him?"

"He killed my brother," Hustle said, throwing the money in the car.

"Damn."

"You worked for him for five years, so you know how shady that old nigga get," Hustle said.

"Fo'sho."

"Hit me up when you ready for me again," Hustle got in his car to leave, unaware that all eyes were on them.

***

Chubs had a big smile on his face, driving into his hood with a trunk full of coke.

Chubs had been working for Will for a few years, but he recently felt like it was time to go his own way and get to a bigger bag. He felt like Will was spoon-feeding him.

Going to Will's opp and number one enemy to buy drugs was the ultimate disrespect and disloyalty.

He knew if Will found out, he was now getting work from Hustle shit could get ugly.

Parking next to his baby mother's car, he snatched the bag as he climbed out.

Chubs started dancing in the middle of the street with the drugs in his right hand.

Walking into his baby mother's crib, she was standing on the couch sniffing coke butt ass naked. Her long saggy titties hung on the table as she sniffed lines of coke.

"Babe," she said.

"You partying without me, boo," he said, walking into the living room.

"I was waiting for you," she lied, lifting her head.

"I can't tell, shawty. You sniffing a whole fucking mountain." He opened the bag filled with keys.

His baby mother peeped in it to see what he had going on in the bag.

"What's that?"

"More money." He put the keys out on the table.

"Shit daddy," she said after seeing all the keys.

"A nigga about to be rich now, believe that," Chubs said, smiling.

BOOM!

The front door flew open, and a masked man entered with a big ass Draco.

"I fucking dare you to move, nigga. I'll blow your shit off little bitch ass nigga!" the gunmen shouted.

Chubs and his baby mother stared at the gun in the man's hand and followed his orders.

The voice somewhat sounded familiar, but Chubs looked past it and prayed for his survival tonight, making it out of this alive.

"You hoe ass nigga. You thought I wasn't going to find out?" The gunmen looked at Chubs before he took off his mask.

"Fuck," Chubs said, seeing it was Will.

"It's a surprise?"

"Nah, Will. It's not what you think. I was trying to find out some info on him, so I could bring it to you," Chubs explained.

"So, that's why you stop picking up your phone?"

"Nah, bruh. I been sick." Chubs was a good liar but Will saw through it all.

Will had his own way of reading people and bringing shit out of someone.

"Sick," Will repeated as he laughed.

"It's not how it looks, dawg. I swear on everything," Chubs said, sweating.

"You sure, bro? I see some keys right there," Will said, pointing to the bricks on the table.

"Oh, that's just some shit I had for a few months."

"Pass me one," Will said.

"Huh?" Chubs said, as his girl picked one up and passed it to him.

Will put his Draco down on the table and cut open the key with a pocket knife. He tasted the white substance and spit it out.

"You dumb, nigga. This sheet rock."

"Hell, nah. That's real. Hustle just -" Chubs realized it was too late as Will fired shots in Chubs and his baby mother.

Boc

Boc

Boc

Boc

Boc

Boc

Boc

Boc

Boc

Boc

Boc

"Mommy!" A little kid came running out of the back room in his pajamas.

Will fired two bullets in the kid's chest by mistake.

Boc

Boc

The little boy's body dropped in the hallway, dying slowly.

"Shit." Will didn't mean to kill the kid, but he got startled and fired first off impulse.

Will left the apartment and went to his car parked up the street. He'd been following Chubs all day.

Getting back in his car, all he could think about was killing that little kid seconds ago for nothing.

"You good?" Banks asked, starting up the Cadillac CTS-V.

"Yes, drive."

"He admitted to it, or was he still lying to his grave?" Banks asked because he disliked Chubs.

Banks was Will's shooter and caps. He took a liking to Banks a few years back when he came home after his second fed bid.

The name Banks came about because he loved robbing banks, so the hood gave him that name.

Working for a boss like Will, he was not worrying about robbing no more banks or nothing. Now he planned to take care of the son and daughter he had by two different women.

"He betrayed us to get betrayed." Will sucked his gold teeth while rubbing his beard. It was something that he did when he was in deep thought.

"What happened?"

"Hustle hit him with an old school move."

"I'm not catching."

"Hustle gave him some real work at first, you know. Blessed his game. Then, when he came back, hit him with some old southern love," Will informed.

"Damn. Hustle got down like that?" Banks asked, driving through the urban ghetto he was raised in.

"No, he don't. So, that only leaves me to believe Hustle is a step ahead of us."

"You saying he knew we would knock Chubs off or find out?" Banks tried to make sense of this.

"Basically."

"He's smarter than we thought."

"We?"

"Well, me," Banks corrected himself.

"Hustle was raised by one of the most successful hustlers to come out of Raleigh."

"Who?"

"His brother Chess," Will added, thinking back to when Chess used to school him on the game.

"I got a question."

"What?" Will tried not to do Chess, but it was hard.

"Why did you kill Hustle's brother if he raised you in the game?" Will asked.

"That's a long story, Banks. That was twenty years ago almost," Will stated seriously, looking out of the car window pulling up to his crib.

"Tell me."

"One day, not today. We had a long night, and I need you to get some sleep. We got a long day tomorrow." Will got out of the car.

"You think Tae going to be ready tomorrow?"

"I don't know, I think so he can be very useful to me," Will answered, getting his Gucci bag.

"Good night, boss," Banks said as Will walked in his home he had for a few years now.

He poured himself a drink and sat on his couch looking at a picture that he took with Chess in Jamaica when he was alive.

Will's mind shifted to Chess as he dozed off.

***

Twenty Years Ago

The Westside of Raleigh was moving so much dope and coke throughout the city, everybody from other cities were coming to cop weight from one person or his worker.

Chess was a big time player in the city and his worker and go to guy was Lil Will.

Tonight there was going to be a big party at a mansion in Durham, but only big time players and boss type niggas attended.

"Lil Will, where you at?" Chess yelled from his living room, fixing his tailor made suit.

"What's up, Chess?" Lil Will came out of the kitchen eating a sandwich.

"You ready for the big party?" Chess asked.

"Yeah, I guess."

"It's going to be a big night for the city," Chess said.

"What you mean?"

"What it sounds like, youngin." Chess turned his attention to him.

"I don't know."

"I'm retiring tonight."

"Why?"

"I'm sixty years old, and I been in this game thirty years. I made millions, and I lived my life," Chess said as he heard a loud BOOM ...

"Get down!" A masked man ran up in the spot, but Chess was quick on the trigger.

Bloc

Bloc

Bloc

Bloc

Chess hit the gunman four times in the chest, knocking him down.

"Grab his gun!" Chess yelled to Lil Will as he stood in front of the gunman.

Chess took off the mask on the man's face, and he saw he was a young man.

Chess tried to recall where he saw the young man's face from before, but he couldn't remember.

"Who sent you? Little bitch nigga Carl and them boys?" Chess asked.

"Him," the gunman said before dying, looking at Lil Will.

Chess looked behind him and saw his young boy with a gun out on him. Lil Will held the gun with both hands.

"Move too fast, and I'll blow your shit off," Lil Will threatened.

"Wow, little nigga. After all the game I showed you."

"You taught me well and showed me the game, but you slipped when you taught me too much," Lil Will said.

"I can only blame myself, I saw it in your eyes youngin."

"True."

"Tonight I was going to retire and give the game to you," Chess said, still shocked about what was going on.

"Why get spoon fed when I can have the whole cake?"

"I'll tell you why, because when you get greedy and full, what will be your next move? Life is like chess. Your next move gotta be your best move," Chess told him.

"I agree, so I'ma kill you, take your gold Rolex, and rob you," Lil Will told him his plans.

"One thing."

"What?"

"Is it worth it?"

"Maybe. I'll see when the time comes, but right now I'll take the risk," Lil Will said.

Bloc

Bloc

Bloc

Bloc

Bloc

Lil Will killed Chess. He walked out of the living room and went to the basement to rob Chess of everything.

Romell Tukes

Chapter 2
North Raleigh, N.C.

Tae was out in his hood in The North Raleigh Projects trying to sell dime bags of low level weed that had seeds in it still, but would still get you high.

His life was a hustle since he dropped out of high school to play the hood with his best friend Justin.

Tae was eighteen and Justin was the same age, the men's birthdays were two days apart.

Tae had two twin sisters and one brother who moved out his mom's house to live with his girlfriend who was now pregnant.

His older brother JD worked a regular 9-5 job to make ends meet. He wasn't a street nigga.

Tae loved his projects, and he ran a tight ship with his young boys who were all around the same age as him.

Tae was a fighter and a shooter. His name was big time in Raleigh because he got caught shooting at police at the age of sixteen, and he beat the case and the one cop ended up dying at the hospital.

Since that happened, his name had been big in the city, but he had a lot of real beef with other hoods.

Tae was of medium height and dark. He had long dreads with big lips, but the women loved him. Especially his sisters friends. His sisters both had a lot of bad high school friends.

Growing up, his mother only had welfare, section 8, and food stamps. His dad wasn't around, he never met him, and he didn't plan to.

His mom didn't work, all she did was drink and chill at her friends' houses, and played cars acting dumb trying to fuck the young hustlers because she still looked decent with a big ass.

"It's hot as hell out here," Justin said, taking off his shirt.

"Fact, bruh."

"I'm sick of selling dimes, bro. We need a come up," Justin said. He leaned on a car that had been in the hood forever.

"Nigga, we need a miracle," Tae joked, but was serious, seeing the hood was dry today.

"How much you got?"

"Forty dollars," Tae said.

"No nigga, I'm talking about how much weed?"

"I got a half ounce, bruh. On deck." Tae dug into his shirt.

"Damn, I ain't even got enough to re-up." Justin shook his head.

"Who dis?" Tae said, looking at a new Audi A8 pull up with rims and tint.

"I don't know, should I get the piece?" Justin asked, ready to shoot because they had wild beef.

"Chill out." Tae saw his uncle's head when the window rolled down.

"Nephew!" Will yelled before he got out of the car.

Tae never really had a real bond with his uncle, but he would see him from time to time and Will would give him a few hundred and give him some wisdom.

His mom disliked him for some reason. He never asked or cared why anyway.

"What's going on?" Tae embraced the man he really didn't know or care for too much.

"You tell me," Will said, looking at Justin who ice grilled him.

"Same ole shit, dawgy."

"I see."

"Nice car," Tae said.

"That can be yours one day. Take a skip with me, cuz," Will said, walking away from his car and Justin.

"What you need to talk about?" Tae questioned.

"Damn. Calm down. I'm here to help you."

"I don't need help. I get it out the mud," he said with his chest out.

"Look, I know you out here tryna do what you do, but let me put you on to some real money," Will said.

"Real money?"

"I'ma make you rich. This project is a goldmine, and I know you and your crew can do big things out here," Will said, seeing Tae think.

"Nah, I don't want no hand out from you my nigga," Tae stated, seeing Justin pass two bags of weed to some young teens.

"Everything you get will be out the mud. I'm not giving you shit cuz you finna take it," Will said.

"Huh?"

"Yeah, you about to get it out the mud, so if you down this Friday at 8 am, meet me at the diner on Main Street."

"I move wit' my gang, bruh."

"The more the better." Will laughed, walking off, getting in his luxury car pulling off.

"What was that about?" Justin asked, watching Will drive out of the lot.

"Your wish been answered," Tae said, still thinking about the convo.

"My wish?"

"My uncle said he knew a way we can get money."

"I don't know, bruh. I'm not selling for no nigga, cuz." Justin got very serious. He wanted no handouts at all.

"It's not like that, cuz."

"I don't get it."

"Me, either. I'ma see what he talking about on Friday, but I think this could be our lick. Call the whole gang. Let them know we may be going on a few drills," Tae said.

"They thirsty for that, but I don't trust your uncle," Justin said.

"Me either, but it's business," Tae said thinking about what his uncle had in store.

Romell Tukes

Chapter 3
Durham, N.C.

Scrilla was deep in a young bitch's pussy in her bedroom making the bed rock and bang against the wall non-stop.

"Ohhh shit!" the brown-skinned woman shouted.

Scrilla was about to bust his nut until the door busted open, and the chick's pops ran inside with a bat in his hand.

The chick jumped up butt ass naked and tried to cover for Scrilla as he got dressed and jumped out of the window.

Scrilla landed in the backyard on the low cut grass and ran to the front of the house.

His heart raced non-stop as he saw the chick's father now outside with a gun in his hand.

Boc

Boc

Boc

Boc

Boc

Boc

Boc

Boc

Boc

Boc

Boc

Scrilla made it to his car, which was an old Impala with a few car problems with it.

When he started it up, he pulled off getting away from the gunfire.

The woman told him her dad was sleeping and was a hard sleeper, but he saw now that was a lie.

Scrilla drove back to his hood on the Northside to tell his crew about what just happened.

Fucking bitches was all he did besides sell pills to fiends and mostly pill heads. He also robbed niggas here and there for his sick hustle.

He ran with a crew of grimy niggas and hot heads from his block on 700 Daud. AKA 700 Block was his click.

700 Block was known for violence and getting money.

Scrilla was a live young nigga who had always been a problem child growing up in a fucked up household.

His mom was a crackhead, and she was strung out on heavy crack and pills.

He barely saw his mom nowadays because she was always in jail or in a rehab center.

Scrilla's grandmom basically raised him and his older sister who now worked for some pimp nigga.

His mom told him his dad was in prison somewhere and hated them so he never came back.

Pulling up to his hood everybody was Blood gang members and G's and a few Crips, but everybody was gang... gang...

Scrilla saw his bestfriend Main was posted up with a white cup full of lean.

Main was a wild careless young nigga who had a trigger finger and a quick temper.

"What's up, bruh?" Main said as he saw a bullet hole in his boy's Impala.

"Man. Bruh, guess what the fuck just happened?"

"What? We gotta slide?" Main asked, ready to kill.

"Nah, peep game. Dawg, I was fucking this little bitch who had some good pussy and her pops bust in."

"Oh, shit. Blood like on some House Party shit," Main said, making four other young niggas laugh.

"Hell, yeah. Bruh, that nigga had his bat at first, but by the time I made it out the window, he was busting at me."

"Let's go ride on that bitch ass nigga."

"Nah, shawty gonna tell," Scrilla said, sitting on a bench.

"Man fucked dat, bruh," Main said, taking a sip of lean in the heat feeling the summer.

"Chill out, we got bigger problems with them 600 niggas," Scrilla said speaking on his opps.

"Facts," one of the young niggas said.

A Cadillac pulled up, and the windows rolled down.

"What's up, cuz?" Will said.

"Will, what's up, cousin?" Scrilla said to his cousin.

Will was Scrilla's cousin, and Will was also moving a lot of weight in the city.

Scrilla also knew Will had a big empire in Raleigh, which was only at least twenty minutes away from each other.

"Take a ride," Will said.

"You good?" Main asked Scrilla.

"Yeah, blood. I'll be back in a few." Scrilla climbed in the car with his cousin.

"How's the family?" Will pulled away from the slums.

"Shit all good, bruh."

"Good, but I got a position for you and your crew," Will said.

"What's that?"

"A chance to make some money," Will stated.

"I make money now."

"Nah, I know a way you can make some money and crush your opps. Them 600 niggas locking down the city, fucking with M.I. and when his brother come home they're going to lock down this whole shit," Will said.

"Give me a few days I'ma get with you, but you may have to put in some work," Will made known.

"That's my middle name," Scrilla said, smiling.

Romell Tukes

Chapter 4
North Raleigh, N.C.

Tae had been thinking about what his uncle said to him a few days ago when he pulled up on him.

Tae needed a new hustle because selling dime bags of dirt weed was not what he pictured the game would be like years ago.

"You straight?" Justin asked as he drove Tae to the Denny's on Wake Forest Road.

"Why you ask?" Tae didn't have a car, but Justin had a beat up hooptie, which was a 1985 Cutlass on its last leg.

"I'm with you, bruh."

"I know. I just hope this nigga know sumthin."

"I asked my man about him, and he said Will getting to a big bag out here and in Durham, but he can't be trusted at all," Justin said, pulling into the Denny's driveway.

"I'ma go up in here and see what's up, bruh. If it don't sound right, I'm not finna put us in no position," Tae said before getting out of the car.

Tae walked into the small restaurant to see only a few people enjoying breakfast that morning.

He saw Uncle Will sitting in the back near the window drinking orange juice looking at him.

"Uncle, what's up?"

"I see you made it. You hungry? I ordered some pancakes already," he said.

"I'ight."

"I see you came out here with our man." Will looked out of the window at Justin in the car parked near his Cadillac.

"Yeah, that's gang."

"You trust him?" Will asked seriously, looking him in his eyes.

"With my life."

"I had a friend who used to say that same shit."

"Where is he now?"

"Dead," Will said.

"How?"

"That's neither here nor there," Will responded as their food arrived.

"I been thinking, and I'm ready to elevate."

"Elevate? Are you sure because you don't even know what's in store," Will said.

"I don't care."

"Ok. Well, I'ma tell you," Will said, looking at him.

"I'ma listen, O.G."

"I want you and your crew to rob some niggas, but the income and profit you and your crew receive from these robberies will be all yours," Will stated.

"Who we have to rob?"

"I'ma have a new opponent for you every other week, but no matter what happens, you can't expose my hands or your hands."

"So, no bare face licks?" Tae asked.

"Hell, no."

"Why?"

"These are regular block hustlers. These are real plugs. If word gets out, shit can get real ugly," Will stated.

"I'ma need some guns."

"Don't worry, I'll have my boy drop off some shit to you in your hood a little later at 7 p.m.," Will said, knowing that wasn't an issue.

"When will it be the first mission?" Tae asked.

"In a few days."

"Aight, I'll be ready."

"I hope so." Will got up leaving a 1,000 on the table for him, which was like 100,000 to Tae. He already made plans to get a Gucci belt.

Tae sat there and finished his meal, thinking about what he just signed up for.

***

Coke Boys

Durham, N.C.

Scrilla was waiting on Will to come through his hood to see what he was talking about.

He knew Will had some shit always up his sleeve to get some money, so he planned to take advantage of the situation.

His niggas were all ready to eat, especially his GD homies who wanted to gang bang all day.

Scrilla saw Will's car pull up near the playground area next to his projects.

Will was supposed to come by around 8 a.m., but he had something else to do, so he had to reschedule it.

"What's up, bruh," Scrilla said.

"You came alone?"

"I'm the only one here ain't I, bruh?"

"I got some shit lined up for you, but it's dangerous."

"How dangerous?"

"Very."

"I love dangerous, cuz," Scrilla bragged.

"Ok. Well, this will be our unlimited test," Will said.

"My goons ready to eat."

"Ok, so this is the plan. I'ma need you to rob a few key players out here."

"In my city?"

"Yeah. Durham, nigga," Will said.

"Damn, who?"

"Does it matter?"

"Not really," Scrilla stated.

"Good. So I'ma have a lick for you at least two to three times a month, playboy."

"Cool."

"I'ma give you a call in a few days just be ready," Will stated.

"Say no more." Scrilla walked off.

Romell Tukes

Chapter 5
Durham, N.C.

M.I. was in the Crabtree Mall with a pretty young redbone. He planned to take her to the hotel later and tear her guts out of her insides.

Shopping was something he did on a regular basis. He wasn't the most handsome nigga, but he got fly.

All he rocked was designer shit and copped the nicest cars. He had the nicest ride in his hood.

He was making over 10 to 15 a day on a bad day and on a good one, he was seeing over 100,000.

M.I. ran a big part of the city. He was one of the main drug suppliers. He had a few workers that were moving a lot of keys.

"Daddy, can you buy me something out the Chanel store?"

"The what store?" M.I. walked through the mall with four big chains hanging from his neck. "Chanel, boo," the redbone woman with the gold grill and phat ass had every nigga in the mall staring at her.

"Spell it," he said.

"Daddy, you know I ain't pass the sixth grade."

"Bitch, the sign right there. You dumb as hell, babygirl." M. I. laughed.

"You right," she said sadly.

M.I. saw he had two missed calls from his brother and his worker calling about the re-up.

A few hours ago, he got his drugs from Atlanta that touched down in his trap.

He would send females out to Atlanta to pick up the orders and drive back to Durham.

M.I. had a lot of enemies in the city, but his #1 enemy was Will. He planned to kill him on sight.

The beef with him and Will went way back, but their history was different from most of his opps.

Will raised M.I. He showed him the game when he was a young teen fresh off the porch.

Will killed M.I.'s real dad that he never knew over a drug debt from years ago.

When M.I. found out it was his big homie who murked his pops, he had a hate for him.

Months after his father's death, he saw Will and fired at him in broad daylight, killing his passenger.

After that, there was beef between the two men.

M.I. left the mall and had to pay a visit to his city, but he wanted to test drive the redbone.

***

Southside Durham
Hours later

City and four of his homies were in the trap filled with bricks that two women just dropped off an hour ago.

City was a young gangsta who ran the GDs on his side of town that he grew up on. City worked for M.I. and YN. The two men showed him the game, but he was loyal to them forever.

Growing up, his mom was a fiend and his dad was a bank robber. His dad was always in and out of jail.

YN raised him, but M.I. put the finishing touching on him.

"Yo, MJ. Take these 15 keys to YN and I'ma wait on the big homie," City told his little cousin.

"You sure?" MJ asked. He was getting up looking at City bag up YN's portion of keys, leaving him ten bricks.

M.I. was taking too long to come, so he thought he should just save him some trouble by sending YN his drugs first.

"Yes."

"Ok, bruh." MJ took the keys and left the crib.

"M.I. never late," B Dog said, looking at his watch.

City called M. I.'s phone to only get the voicemail again, so he put his phone down.

"Man bruh, in another hour we out. I got money to get. I already missed out on 10,000, my nigga," City stated.

The knock at the door startled everybody.

"About time, cuz," B Dog said, getting up to open the door.

"M. I. Here. Ya'll clean that shit up, bro," City told his young boys rolling a blunt on the living room table with weed everywhere.

M. I. hated weed all over the trap because if the police raided the spot, they would use the weed to build a case.

When B Dog opened the door, he was introduced to a bullet to his face and head.

Bloc

Bloc

Bloc

Bloc

Bloc

Bloc

Bloc

Scrilla and his crew shot everybody in the crib and saved City for last.

"Scrilla," City said. He was shocked to see a nigga he used to be cool with.

"Damn, City. You fucked up, bro." Scrilla shook his head.

"Let me live, bruh."

"I can't," Scrilla spoke before pulling the trigger again.

Bloc

Bloc

Bloc

"Snatch all that shit, bruh. We gotta bounce. You hear me," Scrilla told his four man crew who took all the drugs.

Two of his people even dug into the dead men's pockets, looking for money or more drugs.

Romell Tukes

Chapter 6
Raleigh, N.C.

Banks and a little nigga named Spin waited for Tae to come to a Walmart parking lot, so he could give him a bag full of guns.

"Where these dumb ass niggas at?" Bank asked himself.

"Do you even know these Northside niggas?" Spin asked, turning down the car's radio.

"These Will people."

"Oh. You should of said that, my nigga," Spin was Bank's worker.

"Sometimes you talk too much. You just need to listen and pay attention to what's in front of you," said Bank.

A hooptie pulled into the parking lot and parked a few cars near Bank.

"That's dem?"

"Yeah, come on. Grab the bag," Bank ordered as he got out of the car.

***

"I hope these niggas ain't on no bullshit, folk," Justin said, seeing Bank and Spin get out the car.

"If they are, you got that 9mm on you, bruh?" Tae asked.

"Hell, yeah," Justin stated before they got out the car to handle their business with Will's people.

"You Will people, cuz?" Tae asked.

"Yeah, let's make this shit quick," Bank said, giving Spin the signal to pass off the bag.

Spin passed Justin the bag, trying to figure out why he looked so familiar.

"Thanks," Tae said.

"In the bag there is a note for you from Will. Read it good and get back at him. The weapons are on us, cuz," Bank said before walking off.

"'Iight," Tae said, turning to leave.

Justin placed the bag of guns in the backseat of his car.

"That's the little nigga Spin who killed Taz and Kane," Justin said.

"Big Taz?"

"Yeah," Justin stated.

"Damn, he was a problem. That little nigga killed some heavy hitters," Tae said as Justin pulled off.

"Look who he down with."

"True." Tae grabbed the bag, looking inside to see a bunch of guns and a note.

"What that say?" Justin asked, seeing Tae pull out a note.

Tae started to read the note Will left in the bag.

"Listen, nephew. I gave you the guns. Now, it's time for you to put them to use and get it out the mud. There is a man from the Southside named Dread C. He's a big shot nigga who moving a lot of weight in my streets. His baby mother's addy is on the back of the paper, so it's an easy lick, but don't fuck this shit up, please. When you complete this, call me, all the funds is for you and our team. Make sure you have some solid niggas on your team just in case shit goes sour. Be safe ..."

Tae looked at the back of the paper to see an addy below.

"You heard of Dread C from the Southside?" Tae asked Justin who listened to the whole letter also.

"Nah shawty, but we finna find out," Justin added.

***

North Raleigh, N.C.

Dread C drove to his little cousin's house to see how much money he had of his. Driving around on his 32 inch rims on a Chevy was his every day affair on the regular.

Dread C was a bigtime dope boy in the city under Big Zone who was the biggest dope boy in the city besides a man named Will.

He pulled up to the apartment complex and his cousin was already outside with a bag in his hand full of money.

"Here you go, cuz," Dread C's cousin Max said, dropping the bag through the passenger window onto the seat.

"How much is that?"

"Huh?" Max shot back.

"How much is in the bag, bruh? Don't play with me," Dread C stated, opening the bag.

"80,000." Max's voice faded.

"Nigga, where is the twenty thousand that's supposed to go with that?" he asked, knowing there was supposed to be 100,000 in the bag.

"Can I owe you?"

"Max, you play dangerous games, bruh. On everything I love." Dread C got upset because he had to pay Big Zone.

"I'm sorry, but give me a few days. I'll have it."

"Nigga, get the fuck away from my car." Dread C pulled off seeing a text from his baby mother Nikki.

She texted him asking him when he would be home. He texted Nikki back, saying he was minutes away.

When he got to his crib, he placed his long dreads that hung to the floor in a pony, so they wouldn't drag on the floor.

Dread C got his name because he had long dreads, and the C stood for Crip because he was a Crip.

He took the bag and went into his house in the hood.

"Nikki, why you blowing my phone up?" Dread C walked inside the crib looking for her.

Nikki would normally be on the couch watching TV or at least she would act like she was, but she would really be waiting on him.

Dread C couldn't see her, so he made his way to the back room, but when he opened the door, he was shocked.

A young nigga had Nikki bent over fucking her doggie style as she looked like she was enjoying it.

"Yes, more ..." she moaned, not realizing Dread C walked in.

Two men had guns trained on him.

"Bitch, what you doing?"

"Oh, shit." She rolled off the bed as her juices spilled everywhere. The young nigga been fucking her for years. He was

Tae's friend. When she realized it was him she demanded he fuck her before Dread C got there. Nikki knew it was a robbery, but she thought it wasn't serious because she knew Bun.

"Right on time," Tae said with Justin beside him watching Nikki get dressed.

"This is what you want?" Dread C tossed the money on the floor.

"Yeap," Justin said before pulling the trigger on Dread C then Tae killed Nikki.

"Damn, her pussy was good," Bun said.

"Nigga, get the bag. We out freak, nigga," Justin said, leaving.

Chapter 7
South Durham, N.C.

Today was City's funeral, and it was the talk of the town. City had a lot of love throughout Durham and other cities on the outside.

Main and Scrilla drove through the city in a low-key rental with tint on the windows. They had two shooters in the back cleaning Tech 9 cub machine guns.

Word in the street was YN had a bag on City killer's head and wanted to know who killed his little homie.

"How you want to go about this shit, dawg?" Main asked Scrilla.

"What you mean?" Scrilla questioned, driving past a store where a gang of young niggas stared the car down.

"How you trying to play this shit, bruh?" Main asked knowing Scrilla was feeling a certain type of way because he hated when niggas called him out.

He felt like by YN putting money on his head, he wasn't about to let niggas have him hide out. His pride was too big.

"Follow my lead."

"You know what this shit can lead to right?" Main asked.

"Yeah, I'm ready for all dat smoke, bro," Scrilla said, pulling into the graveyard to see rows of cars lined up.

"Da gang ready for whatever, but niggas still got that work at the trap," Main said.

The drugs they got from City were stashed in the trap house because he wanted a solid plan to lock shit down on the drug side.

Scrilla preferred to rob niggas rather than sell drugs because selling work was too much of a headache.

"We finna get situated once we done with this shit. Park right there, bruh," Main said, putting on his bulletproof vest.

They saw a crowd of people crying and hugging one another as the funeral got wrapped up.

"Everybody stay low and cover for me while I try to take this nigga mama out," Scrilla spoke.

"His mom?" one of the little niggas said from the backseat.

"Send a message." Scrilla hopped out with his crew.

When they got out of the car, they bum rushed the funeral running to the crowd.

Tat...

Tat...

Tat...

Tat...

Tat...

Tat...

Tat...

Tat...

People scattered all over the place, scared to death as the four men sprayed into the crowd clearing the path.

City's mother heard the shots and ran to the nearest tree, thinking she was safe, until Justin and his crew closed in on her, firing a few bullets in her face.

Scrilla knew City's mom. She used to sell five dollar plates of food in the hood and she had a phat ass. He used to love seeing her in jeans.

Once she laid dead, they left, leaving two more civilians dead at the gravesite.

***

YN and his crew were on their way inside the funeral entrance when they heard gunshots and saw cars flying past them to live.

"We out," YN told the driver of the SUV, not knowing what was going on.

"What the fuck!" the driver yelled as he backed up and saw cars coming from all over the place in a panic.

YN's phone rang and he picked it up. It was a little bitch he used to fuck.

"What?" YN answered.

"They just shot up City's funeral," the woman reported.

"Who?"

"Lil Scrilla and Main," she replied.

"Who da fuck is that?" YN asked before the phone went dead.

YN grew up in Durham and started fucking with M. I. on the money tip, and now he was up. Being young and hood rich, YN lived a fast life.

Running around with a nigga like M. I., he knew he would become rich and famous like him. Getting g-money was all he knew since a kid, he watched niggas around him get money and kill shit.

Watching everything growing up, he became attracted to this lifestyle, and now he was trying to put his 600 crew on.

Romell Tukes

Chapter 8
Southeast, Raleigh

Tae split the eighty thousand dollars up with Justin and his boy, Bun. Tae had no clue Bun knew Dread C's girl Nikki, the crazy part was she begged him to fuck her.

With his uncle putting him on licks, he knew sooner or later something would backfire, but until then, Tae planned to get money.

He was in an Uber on his way to a used car dealership to cop a used car for the low. After this, he was going to meet his uncle to talk about whatever he had on his mind.

Tae got 27,000 from the robbery, and he put 17,000 up in a shoebox for rainy days.

Justin copped a new BMW car. He went crazy, but Tae knew Justin never had shit before, so blowing his first little bag was understandable.

Pulling into the car lot, he saw a black Nissan and a white Toyota.

"Thanks," Tae said, as he paid for the Uber before hopping out.

Walking into the lot, he saw one of the workers and approached her. She was a big girl with an ugly face and funny shaped body.

"Those two cars are for sale?" he asked.

"Yeah."

"How much?"

"For you cutie, 9,500," the woman said, dropping five hundred dollars.

"Ok. How do I get tags and shit?" Tae looked at both of the cars, trying to figure out which one he wanted.

"I can give you some temp tags until you get your plates, but which car you want, though?" she asked.

"Give me the Nissan," he said.

"Ok."

"Thank you."

"Give me a second." She walked off.

Tae couldn't believe he was about to get his first car. He felt good about it.

The Dread C robbery went good, but Tae knew from here on shit could get dirty.

Tae never had shit in his life, and he planned to run it up once he got the money.

He wanted to put some money into the streets, so his people could eat and get on.

One thing he learned from other people's downfalls was to feed the wolves before they eat you. Having a crew full of young hungry niggas could be his elevation or downfall.

Minutes later, the fat bitch came out of the back with keys, papers, and license plates for him.

"How you going to pay?"

"Cash."

"Good, anything under 10,000 is good enough to keep the feds out of your affairs," she said.

"That's good to know," he said, handing her the money from the Dread C robbery.

"Thanks. Enjoy your new ride." She walked off.

Tae started to do his money dance, and then he put the tags on the car. It was only a Nissan, but it was still something to him.

***

North Raleigh, N.C.

Uncle Will waited in the Pizza Express spot, eating the best pizza in Raleigh. He waited for his nephew to show up, so he could put him on game to another dope boy.

He heard about Dread C. He was impressed with his nephew's work, how he handled it like a true gangsta.

Will's phone was going off. It was the client in Winston who wanted 40 keys, but Will had to go out to South Carolina tonight.

He texted Bank and told him to go holla at Wooh because he was busy today.

A black Nissan pulled up to the restaurant and Tae hopped out, blasting music.

Will could never figure out why the young generation loved attention and blasting music was alerting the police to him.

"Uncle, what's up?" Tae sat down as Will offered him a slice of pizza.

"You did a good job."

"Thanks."

"Where is my cut?" Will asked seriously, seeing he caught Tae off guard.

"I got it at home," Tae lied. He really forgot about Will.

"That's for you, bruh. Enjoy yourself, but for the next few missions I want you and your crew to live it up and get on your feet."

"That's what's up, dawg." Tae saw the distrust in his uncle's eyes.

"I got a young nigga named Glass from the Westside I need you to go see."

"Glass from where on the west?" Tae heard of the name.

"Kingwood Projects."

"How do I supposed to get up in there?" Tae knew for a fact them Kingwood niggas be having niggas all in and out on post over there.

"Figure it out."

"Iight." Tae got up.

"You're on your way to the top. Trust me, you gonna have a bright future but the first thing I need you to do is get your own crib somewhere to duck off because bodies are about to drop soon, and I want you to be smart," Uncle Will stated.

"I know," Tae said as he got up to leave.

Romell Tukes

Chapter 9
Southside, Durham

M.I. got an urgent call from YN asking him to meet him near Enterprise Projects, a section where the Bloods gang members controlled.

YN had the hood flooded with drugs and guns.

Business been on the up and up lately shit been going perfect but at the moment he had one big issue and that was Will.

When he got the news of his little nigga City's death, he flipped out because that was his man and he owed him some money.

M.I. saw YN's truck parked at the gas station near the projects and got out.

"YN what up, dawg?" M.I. said as he took his time getting out of the car.

M.I. looked at YN's face, and he knew something was wrong, he just couldn't pinpoint the shit.

"These fuck niggas shot up City funeral, bruh!" YN shouted.

"Hold up, when was this shit?" M.I. asked.

"The other day. You ain't hear about da shit?"

"Nah, I was out of town. What happened and who the fuck we gotta kill?" M.I. got serious.

"I drove to little bruh funeral and on my way there I see niggas flying out in a panic like there was a bomb in that bitch."

"Oh, shit." M.I. made all types of sound effects.

"These little niggas shot the funeral up and killed City's mom," YN said sadly because he knew City's mom. She was a good southern lady.

"Who was the little niggas?"

"Scrilla and Little Main," YN said, knowing Main, but not so much Scrilla.

"Kill dem hoe ass niggas. Put a bag on their head."

"Nah, I want to handle this shit."

"At least we know who killed bru now," M.I. said.

"Yeah, I'ma handle it."

"It may be deeper than what we see, you know."

"That makes sense. I'ma figure it out," YN said, turning to leave, thinking about his new victims.

***

Miami, Fl

Hustle and two badass strippers drove on jet skis on a Miami Beach enjoying the weekend.

Hustle needed a small vacation, so he got out of North Carolina for a weekend, something he rarely did.

There was one nigga on his mind day and night, which was Will. Every time he heard his name in the streets, it made his blood boil.

The streets had a strong hold on Hustle, but he knew his life wouldn't last forever.

Hustle was gettin a big bag in N.C. and S.C. He had a few traps doing numbers. He also had a few legit businesses under his belt.

Growing up, he got the name Hustle because all he did was sell candy in the school and hustle niggas.

His brother Chess was one of the smartest niggas he'd ever met in his life. He showed him the game in and out.

Chess taught him how to be a lion and snake in the jungle. When Hustle lost his brother, his life went for a left turn.

When Chess got killed, Hustle got arrested for a murder case he ended up beating. He was a teenager back then when he caught the body. Luckily, he beat the odds, turned his case over, and went home.

Coming home, he got into the field and started fucking with his brother's old plug.

Before Chess' death, they had a long talk about Will and how Chess didn't trust him.

Chess also told him if something was to happen to him, Will would be the cause because he had envy in his heart and jealousy.

Hustle got off the jet skis and looked at the thick black queens he had with him enjoying themselves.

"Y'all want to go shopping?" he asked both women.

"Hell, yeah. Can we get some Birkin bags?" one of them asked.

"If you suck and fuck me good," he answered.

"That goes without question, daddy," the other woman said, pulling the thongs out her big ass.

"Ok," Hustle said, walking off the beach on to the boardwalk, seeing males and females eyeing the girls.

Hustle loved women. He was always with two or three hoes. This was the life he felt like he deserved.

***

Rocky Mountain, N.C.

Bri worked as a bartender in a local club/gentlemen's club. She was the youngest bartender in the club. At nineteen, Bri was fully developed and looked sexy.

She stood five-six, thick, hazel eyes, and nice C cup breasts. She looked like she belonged in a magazine or on TV.

Bri had a twin sister named Tajara who looked just like her, but she was slim. Her twin sister was in college in Atlanta in her freshman year. If she would have gone to college with her sister, she would have been a freshman.

College wasn't for her. She was a natural born hustler into making money.

Years ago if someone would have told her she would be working in a club, she would laugh, but it wasn't a joke now because she had bills to pay. Bri recently moved into a two-bedroom apartment with a female friend. Bri wanted a new hustle because this wasn't it at all.

Romell Tukes

Chapter 10
Raleigh, N.C.

Tae arrived at the downtown jail to see his favorite cousin, Low Dee, who was locked up for an attempted murder charge.

That day, Low Dee shot a nigga on camera in a shopping center in front of Tae. The dude he shot ended up snitching on Low Dee, and shit went bad from there.

Hours after Low Dee shot the nigga, the police kicked in Low Dee's baby mother door at his mom's crib where they found him in the basement.

Tae and Low Dee were first cousins and close since kids.

Low Dee had been sitting in the jail close to eight months now waiting on a good plea deal because the first one was too hard on him.

The DA offered him twenty years on his first offer because of his rap sheet, but he was trying to get it down to twelve years.

Going through the process in the jail visit room area was annoying, but he knew every jail had its own strict rules.

Tae was sent into a room filled with tables and chairs. Prisoners wore jail uniforms as they visited their loved ones.

Looking around, he prayed he didn't see prison. That was his only fear. He knew what came with living a life of violence and negativity.

Later on, he planned to do some research on Kingwood Projects, so he could start planning his new mission.

Low Dee came out of the door in chains and shackles on his ankles, with two guards on the side of him.

"What's up, bruh," Low Dee said as he smiled seeing his cousin.

"I'm good, what happened?" Tae asked, seeing a lump on his head.

"I got into a fight with police. They jumped me and fucked me up, but I put one of them in the fucking hospital!" Low Dee shouted loud enough so one of the guards could hear him.

Tae knew his cousin used to be a hothead since a kid, so nothing he did would surprise him at all.

"You gotta chill out, bruh."

"Fuck all dat. I'm fighting for my life in here, bruh," Low Dee stated, seriously checking out his surroundings, something he did in prison.

"What the courts talking about?" Tae asked.

"I'm trying to get twelve years. Niggas talking about twenty years. Fuck all dat shit, my nigga."

"Damn."

"It's cool but what's up with you, bro? I heard you not in school or nothing, little nigga."

"I'm doing me," Tae said.

"Dang, that will land you in here for life, playboy," Low Dee said because he knew a lot of niggas stuck in jail with life sentences.

"I'm not coming to jail."

"You got a job? Are you fucking with your boy Justin with the weed game?" Low Dee knew Tae was too smart to be trapped off in the hood.

"Nah, I got something else going on."

"What's that?"

"I'm fucking with Uncle Will," Tae said.

Low Dee got quiet for a minute and leaned back, trying to make sense of all this. He didn't trust Uncle Will at all. He saw him snake a lot of niggas when he was out.

He didn't think Tae should deal with Will, but he knew Will would easily put Tae on to some money, but the problem was what came with it.

"Just be careful with him, please, Tae."

"I'm always on point."

"Hope so, but he be in Durham a lot fucking with our cousin," Low Dee stated.

"We got family out there?" Tae asked.

"Yeah, some nigga named Scrilla," Low Dee told him.

"Scrilla?"

"Yeah, I met him a few times. He's cool people, folk," Low Dee said.

"Iight. What's good with your mom and dem?"

"Dey be coming to see me from time to time."

"Ok, that's love," Tae said.

"Yeah, she's getting old, but she's a trooper."

"Your mom cool as a fan."

"I already know, but peep game. I'ma write you a letter soon but come back soon," Low Dee said, knowing the visit was about to end.

"Iight."

"Be safe and keep your eye on Will, just because a nigga says he's family don't make him blood," Low Dee said.

"Love you," Low Dee said.

"Love you too," Tae said, leaving.

Romell Tukes

Chapter 11
Raleigh North, N.C.

Justin pulled into the same projects he grew up in and loved with a passion. North Raleigh projects were full of killers, drug dealers, violence, and poverty.

Growing up, all he knew was get money. In school, when the teacher asked him what he wanted to be, he told them Big Meech.

Seeing niggas in his hood sell a ton of dope and get money made him see life from a different view. He dropped out of school early because he knew that street smarts would take him further than book smarts.

Justin's mom was a crackhead who was barely home because she would be out chasing drugs. His older brother lived with his new girlfriend and they both worked at Best Buy.

His little sister was still in high school, so he did his best to look after her. She was only seventeen, a little younger than him.

Justin was a part of a gang early in his life, starting at the age of twelve. He was down with the Bloods.

"Yooo, Justin!" an older woman yelled coming out of a building, scratching her arm.

The woman used to babysit him as a kid until she started smoking crack and going back and forth to jail for petty offenses.

"What's up, sassy?" Justin closed his car door, slamming it. He had enough money to get a new car, but he wanted to save some money, so he could get his own crib.

Justin hated living in the projects, even though he and his crew ran the whole projects.

"You seen ya mama?"

"Nah, why? What she do now?" Justin asked, knowing his mom did some bullshit as always.

"She stole my flat screen TV and my bracelet the other night. I was out of town for my mom's funeral," Sassy said, pissed off.

"How you know she did?"

"Everybody saw her and that nigga Malcolm leaving my house with it and I know your mom," Sassy said.

Justin knew his mom was that type. She stole from him so many times that he lost count.

"Damn," he said.

"If she don't bring my shit back, I'm calling the police on her ass," she said, placing a hand on her frail hip.

"Here." Justin pulled out a wad of money and peeled off eight hundred dollars for her.

"Where you get all dat from?" Sassy stared at the money as her mouth got watery.

"That's none of your business, but that should cover the cost. Sassy for one, you dead wrong trying to call da police like you don't smoke crack or never been to jail. You not no civilian," he told her.

"I don't steal."

"Whatever." Justin turned to walk off. His building was a few doors down.

"How about you come over later and spend some of that money. I'll make it worth it," she said.

Justin heard how good Sassy's head and pussy was, but he also heard she was the queen of giving niggas STDs even some shit niggas never heard of.

"I'll pass."

"You sure? I'll suck your dick so good you'll be trying to climb through my window at night," Sassy stated.

"No, thanks." Justin walked off.

Once inside his crib, he saw his mom at the kitchen table stuffing pieces of crack into a glass pipe as if she was in a hurry.

"Mom!" he yelled, scolding her.

Justin tried to hide the crack all over the place.

"Your daughter will be home from school in an hour," he said.

"I know, boy. This my damn house!" Sierra shouted.

"Iight."

"Give me some money," she demanded, staring at his pockets.

"What money?"

"Don't play dumb, nigga," she said.

"Why you steal Sassy's TV, Mom?"

Sierra looked at him like he was dumb.

"Nigga, that dumb bitch left her door unlocked. She's lucky I ain't steal more shit. Fuck that stank ass bitch!" Sierra shouted, getting loud.

"I thought she was your friend."

"Ain't no friends in this game. It's every man for self. You know that. You think when shit gets real, your little crew gonna lay fair? If so, you're dumber than you look." Sierra laughed before going to the back where her room was.

Justin paid his mom no mind. He knew she was miserable. He wondered if Tae had another lick set up for them because with his next check, he wanted to move away from his crazy mom.

Romell Tukes

Chapter 12
Clark Atlanta University, ATL

Tajara and her roommate were getting ready to go out to a party on campus. It was Saturday, and this was the only time Tajara had fun because of her busy lifestyle.

College life was crazy for Tajara. She was jam packed with tests and exams. Study hall took two hours out of her time every day, then she had a part-time job at the Atlanta downtown library.

Working and school drained her, but she had to stay focused on becoming a paralegal. Studying the law was something she always wanted to do, and now her dream was coming true.

Tajara was a pretty dark-skinned woman, slim built, long Indian hair, medium sized breasts, and a cute face. She was the wifey type. She had self-respect, loyalty, and she had only been with one man during her nineteen years on earth.

She didn't put herself in any type of sexual relationship with men because she had to focus on school and herself as a woman.

Coming from Raleigh, N. C. she was somewhat new to Atlanta, unlike her roommate who was born and raised in Atlanta, GA.

Her brother Tae and family were stuck in Carolina, but she wanted to really expand her life and shoot for the stars.

Since a kid, her goal was to get out of the city of Raleigh and become successful.

"Tajara, what are you wearing tonight?" Georgia asked, coming out of the shower with a towel wrapped around her.

Georgia was a thick chick with short hair and tattoos all over her lower body. She was from Zone 1 in Atlanta.

"I got a Louis Vuitton dress."

"Good, wear that."

"You sure?" Tajara disliked being too exposed. She liked for men to respect her. Not slap her ass and call her out of her name.

Tajara didn't like the attention from men like her friend Georgia did. Everywhere they went, she had to have eyes on her.

"I'ma get you some dick tonight, bitch. Watch," Georgia said, walking in the room to get dressed for the party.

Tajara shook her head, thinking about her crazy sister Bri, who FaceTimed her almost every day. The two used to be close until she came to Atlanta for school.

Hearing Bri was a bartender made her want to do better, not only for herself, but also for her family.

Going to school was the best choice she ever made in life, and she was blessed. Her grades were always A's and B's of course, nothing less.

Tajara got ready and went out. She didn't drink or smoke, so she focused on dancing and having fun.

***

Raleigh, N.C.

Kingwood Projects was on the Westside of the city and one of the worst neighborhoods in the city.

The projects had one way in and one way out. There was so much money in one little area. There was more than enough to go around.

Everybody from Kingwood was copping drugs from Glass or his brother Rags, who just came home from the feds.

Today there was a big cookout in the projects to pay respects to a Kingwood legend named OG Fatty who was killed by police two years ago in front of his building.

Everybody was posted up under the large gazebo behind the projects and the basketball court.

There was a six on six basketball game going on with a live DJ playing music and kids having fun on the playground.

Glass was with his goons to the far left drinking and shooting dice with Rags, his brother.

At 6'4, Glass was a big boy. He used to ball hard until he found a plug named Will. When shit went wrong with Will, he found a new plug.

Will was taxing him on product, and he got word Will was fucking one of his baby mothers. Glass had six baby mothers and nine kids in all. He felt like Will broke the trust code, and he always heard rumors of how he was a snake. Now Glass was fucking with Hustle and his crew.

"I'ma go to the car. I ran out of paper, dawg," Glass said, walking off from the crowd, making his way to his car. Glass loved shooting dice. It was a habit. Sometimes he would have a hundred bands, and sometimes he would lose more in one roll.

He was drinking all morning, and now it was 12 p.m. When he got to his car, he didn't see the commercial van pulling up on him from behind until it was too late.

Three men hopped out with guns and put their guns to his face, forcing him in the van and racing off before anybody saw them.

Romell Tukes

Chapter 13
North Raleigh, N.C.

The van pulled into an empty lot next to a park where Tae normally hung out. Tae brought this idea up to Justin late notice, but he was down for the lick.

Tae and Justin brought two men with them on this mission, just in case shit got out of hand.

Kingwood had a one-way entrance, so he knew he had to come up with a solid plan. He knew that today there was going to be a big cookout, so he waited in the cut with his goons.

"Park at the end of the lot," Tae told one of his goons from his hood.

"Iight," his boy SL said.

"What's going on, bruh?" Glass' voice was trembling.

"Where the money at?" Tae asked with his A70 pump shotgun 12 gauge pointed at Glass' face.

"It's at my baby mama's crib on Martin Street," Glass said, naming the street of one of the goons in the van.

"We gotta slide over there, bruh," Justin stated.

"Drive over there and if that shit ain't there we finna kill your hoe ass," Tae said.

"I swear on everything I love. The money is in the crib and the coke," Glass told them all, trying to see if he saw any recognizable faces.

They drove to Martin Street and Glass told them to pull over at the tan and gray two-story house in the middle of the block.

"That's it?" Justin asked, scooting out of the crib. They see a familiar Cadillac SUV parked over near a driveway entrance.

"My baby mother is in there. Please don't hurt her," Glass asked, knowing how easily a home invasion could quickly turn into a murder scene.

"Ya'll stay in here wit dis nigga, dawg," Tae stated, getting out of the van with Justin.

"Let's try the front door first and if that shit don't work, we ring the doorbell," Justin stated.

"light. Let's hurry up, it's broad daylight, bro," Tae said, stepping up the steps making it to the top.

Justin turned the loose doorknob and made his way inside the house to hear loud moans.

When they both walked further into the crib, they saw a young nigga on the couch getting his dick sucked by Glass' naked thick baby mother.

Tae and Justin knew who the nigga was an opp, they both looked at each other and fired shots at the man's head.

Boc...

Boc...

Boc...

Boc...

Bullets hit the back of the man's head, killing him as Glass' baby mother jumped up screaming butt ass naked.

"Where the stash at?" Tae said, seeing her point at the closet in the living room a few feet away from her.

Justin went to the closet and quickly found the pillowcase filled with drugs and money.

"We out of here, bruh," Tae said as he saw pee rolling out of the bitch's hairy coochie.

"Ewwww," Justin said.

"Sorry, I'm so scared," she said as she covered her mouth, trying to hold back her tears.

"You good, shawty," Tae said, leaving the crib, but Justin wasn't about to chance it.

Boc...

Boc...

Tae looked back to see Glass' baby mother with two bullets in her face.

"I had to," Justin said, leaving the crib, walking back to the van where he heard screams.

There slid open the slide doors to see Glass crying and screaming. Glass heard the gunshots and knew it was over for her. He loved his baby mother with all his heart.

Tae knew it was the best time to leave Glass there.

Boc...
Boc...
Tat...
Tat...
They tossed Glass out of the van and shot him a few more times before they drove off.

***

Durham, N.C.

Scrilla sat in his car waiting on his Uncle Will to show up and speak to him.

Shit had been crazy lately and his name had been going crazy in Durham, especially after City's funeral that they shot up.

Word on the street was YN was looking for him and wanted him dead.

Scrilla really ain't give a fuck, but he liked to be on point, so knowing YN wanted him dead made it so much easier for him to plot on his opps.

He saw his uncle pull into the pizza lot and got out, looking around. It was getting dark out, but it was still hot outside.

"Nephew." Will hopped out of his car with a big smile.

"Who dat?" Scrilla asked, looking at his drive spin in the driver's seat.

"My bodyguard, but peep game. I heard what you did, and I like how you handled that, but now you have a bigger problem," Will stated.

"I ain't worried, but my hood need some work."

"We will get to the drugs later, but first you need to pull up on YN and M.I. little brother. That's a free lick," Will said.

"M.I. little brother?"

"Yes, here is his info. I'll let you handle the rest, and trust me. After this, you will have a good amount to flood your hood until you ready for me," Will handed him a piece of paper and walked back to his luxury car.

Romell Tukes

Chapter 14
Raleigh, N.C.

Tae went to the fair grounds to attend the fair that always came out to the city once a year. The fair lasted two weeks and the whole city came out to show support, while some came out for other reasons.

Every year, there was some type of violence after the fair. Two years ago, six people got shot and three dead. That mass shooting almost made the fair hard to come back.

Tae had close to twenty goons with him strapped up, just in case some shit popped off. Niggas was click tight there, everybody rolled in large packs tonight.

Since fucking with his Uncle Will, he had been seeing real money. He was saving money, and his goons were seeing a little bread, too.

Walking past a cotton candy stand, he saw a bad brown slim chick with a nice round ass. Her hair was in a bun. He wanted to see her face, so he told his goons he'd catch up with them. Tae knew how sheisty his crew was. If they saw him talking to a chick, they would pull up and say some disrespectful shit. He waited in line behind the woman purchasing the cotton candy.

"Excuse me, what type of cotton candy is that?" Tae asked the woman as she turned around to see who was behind her.

"Huhhh ..." the young woman turned around to see Tae smiling.

"What's the best kind?" Tae asked.

"Oh, bubblegum. It's the pink one," the chick said, holding hers in her hand.

"Thanks. What's your name?" Tae was staring at her beauty.

"Rena."

"I'm Tae."

"Ok, Tae. Nice meeting you, but I have to go. My girls are waiting on me," Rena said, pointing at the group of girls.

"I wanna see you again," Tae told her.

"Me?"

"Yes."

"You don't even know me," Rena shot back.

"That's why I want to take you on a date, so I can build with you and see if we got things in common," Tae said, seeing she was buying it.

"Ok, take my number," she said and gave him her phone number.

"Iight," Tae said, seeing his crew having words with another crew near a rollercoaster.

When she put her number in his phone, he told her bye and rushed to his crew's aid.

"What up, cuz?" Tae walked through the crowd. Now face to face with an older cat with a gold grill.

"What's good, bruh?" The man leading the opposite crew with the grill in his mouth asked.

"You tell me, bruh. We got a problem?" Tae spoke up as his savages were reaching for their guns, ready to air the place out at the slightest head nod.

"Your crew was ice grilling my crew, so my niggas stood on ten toes," the man said.

"So there's no problem?" Tae asked, looking the man in his eyes.

"I hope not," the man replied, who was a few feet taller than Tae.

"Let's slide," Tae said looking at his crew, seeing police all over the place.

When the crowd broke up, Tae stepped to one of his niggas he came there with who knew everybody.

"Who was dat nigga?"

"Big Choppa from Martin Street, he work for Big Zone, his cousin," Tae's soldier responded.

"Oh, yeah. Big Choppa, huh?" Tae looked back to see Big Choppa mean muggin him.

***

Southeast, Raleigh

Spin and Bank walked out of the safe house that Will used to keep drugs in. Will had houses he used to hide money, drugs, guns, and even dead bodies.

"Since when you started riding bikes, cuz?" Bank asked after seeing a blue motorcycle next to his truck.

"It's summertime, bro. I like to feel free." Spin hopped on the bike with no helmet on his head.

"Don't forget we gotta go to Greensboro tomorrow," Bank told Spin before climbing in his truck.

"Iight." Spin got on his bike doing a wheelie. He loved doing stunts on the bike. He was one of the best.

When Spin got a few blocks away, a cop car came out of the cut, flashing its lights because he didn't have on a helmet.

Spin stopped and pulled to the curb, looking behind him as he put a blue flag on his face. When the officer got out of the car to give him a ticket, bullets hit the cop in his face and neck.

Boc... Boc... Boc... Boc... Boc... Boc... Boc... Boc....

Spin emptied the clip on him before racing off again, leaving the ten-year vet on the ground bleeding out of his neck.

Romell Tukes

Coke Boys

Chapter 15
Durham, N.C.

Moez resided on the eastside of the city in a project called Da Mack filled with dangerous gang members known for shooting police and rival gangs.

The hood was run by Moez. He supplied the projects he grew up in since a kid.

Moez was M.I.'s younger brother, who could have been a football player with his 6'5 height and 380 pound frame.

Today was Moez's birthday, and he just came from a club with two of his soldiers he knew since childhood. Flooding the hood with keys brought a lot of attention from the police and opps trying to get a piece of what he had.

"Drop me off, folk," Moez said as the Audi truck came to a stop in front of his side bitch's crib.

Moez kept drugs and money at his side bitch Jessica's crib who was an ex dancer.

"Iight. We'll see you tomorrow, big bruh. Can you make it to the door?" Sean asked who was Moez's best friend.

"Call me." Moez opened the door and got out of the truck, about to stumble.

"Don't drown in that pussy. You know she be putting a spell on niggas," Horse said as he thought back to the time he used to fuck Jessica until Moez wifed the thot.

"Fuck you ..." Moez slurred, throwing up his middle finger, walking to the front door, fumbling in his pockets for the crib keys he had.

Moez paid Jessica's bills and took good care of her. He wasn't a cute nigga, so he had to trick off on other women.

Inside it was dark as always. He walked to the back, thinking how he couldn't wait to fuck her all over the crib.

Walking by the bathroom, he thought he saw something move.

"Whack!!" An A70 pump shotgun 12 gauge busted Moez's face open as he fell to the floor.

"Ahhhhhahh ..." Moez's right eye socket quickly enlarged.

"Get your bitch ass up," Scrilla said as three of his goons came out of the back room with Jessica blindfolded and tied up.

One of Scrilla's ex-girls knew Jessica and was talking to Scrilla about her on FaceTime. She told Scrilla he should trick on her as Moez tricked on her girl Jessica.

"Who are you?" Moez asked, seeing Jessica tied up.

"Fuck all dat, dawg. Where the shit at? I searched dis bitch up and down and got nothing. You feel me?" Scrilla said, forcing his gun to Moez's swollen face.

"It's in the washing machine in the kitchen." Jessica spoke up because she knew Moez would play dumb.

Moez used to always tell her if anybody had the balls to rob him, he would never give up his drugs or money, they would have to kill him.

She saw things a different way. Money was something a person could always get back, but when a person's life is gone, there is no coming back.

"You dumb bitch!" Moez shouted so loud, Jessica jumped out of fear and so did Scrilla's goons.

"Watch him," Scrilla told his crew before he walked off and made his way into the kitchen, where he saw roaches having meetings on the counter tops.

Scrilla opened the washing machine to see stacks of money wrapped up in plastic, and a few were square keys. A big smile appeared on his face as he took everything out of the washer.

Within seconds, he was back in the living room hallway, where Jessica was crying and Moez's face was leaking blood.

"M.I. gonna turn up the city behind this, cuz. That's my fucking brother, you fucked up." Moez saw Scrilla crack a smirk.

"You really are as dumb as you look," Scrilla said.

BOOM!
BOOM!
BOOM!
BOOM!
BOOM!

The shotgun blast tore through Moez's body, each blast almost ripping him in half.

"What about her?" one of his young boy's asked, looking at Jessica.

"Leave her, bruh. Let's go before the police come. She won't say a word except she was sleep. Right, Jessica Thomas, who has a daughter named KiKi that lives with her mom in Bragtown?" Scrilla said, letting her know he had all of her info if she did snitch.

"I saw nothing. I swear I'm still sleep," Jessica stated.

"Iight." Scrilla and his crew walked out with the money and drugs.

Main waited outside in a stolen van, checking out the scene the whole time.

Scrilla had been waiting on Moez for an hour. He saw on social media that today was his birthday, so he knew tonight would be easy, but he knew now M.I. would be on alert.

"Everything straight, bruh?" Main asked, seeing his crew rush back in the van with their arms full of money and drugs.

"Yeah, fool. Drive," Scrilla said, seeing nosy neighbors come outside because of the loud gunshots.

***

North Durham, N.C.

M.I. got the call at 3:40 a.m. about his brother's death and his phone ain't stop ringing yet. The news of Moez's murder hit him hard because he knew Moez wasn't supposed to be in the game. He was supposed to be in the NFL.

The city's been crazy since City was killed and M.I. only saw one connection and that was that Scrilla kid.

Niggas in Bull City, which was Durham's nickname knew better than to try his people because he would clear out a whole block.

M.I. couldn't even go to sleep, and tomorrow he had a meeting with his plug.

Romell Tukes

Chapter 16
Raleigh, N.C.

Big Choppa checked his Rolex watch that hugged his fat wrist.

"Yo, Thirty. I got you later," Big Choppa said to his little Crip homie they called Thirty.

"When, bruh? I only got ten grams left and it's the first of the month," Thirty said, throwing his hands in the air.

"Nigga, who fault is that?"

"You right bruh, but I had to get a new phone," Thirty shot back.

"I'ma go pick up some shit from Raw and dem."

"When you coming back?"

"Later." Big Choppa hated the first. He was a very busy man, especially every first of the month.

Big Choppa was a part of his big cousin's crew, Big Zone. Since his cousin Big Zone had most of the city on lock, he was able to eat off his plate as well.

Big Choppa had his own team of young hitters, controlled by his little brother.

At only eighteen years old, Raw was heavy in the streets.

Big Choppa made his way to Martin Street where one of his traps was and Raw ran it. He kept a lot of work over there, and that was the spot where he had his crew cook the coke.

***

Martin Street, Raleigh

"Yo, Raw! Turn that shit down, bro!" Ice yelled from in the kitchen, where he was on the stove whipping coke.

Raw, Ice, Matt, and Cass were in the trap chilling as usual waiting for Big Choppa to come back, so they could make moves.

It was the first, and they had shit to do selling weight.

"My nigga how long you finna be on stove, bruh?" Raw asked, smoking a blunt of exotic weed.

"I been in dis bitch since 6 a.m. boy you trippin, cuz," Ice shot back sweating into the pot.

"Man, y'all need to hurry up. I gotta --" Matt's words were cut short when the house door got kicked in like it was a police raid.

Everybody looked at the gunmen and quickly realized they weren't police, but jack boys.

Ice went for the FN on his hip, but the MP11 assault rifle stopped him.

Tae and Justin aired all four men out, killing them all easily.

"We gotta hurry. The duffle bags right there," Justin said, putting two more bullets in Ice's head before stepping over him.

Tae bagged up all the drugs in a matter of seconds and left nothing behind.

***

When Big Choppa pulled up to Martin Street, the first thing he saw was four young niggas pacing in front of his trap with Draco's out in the open.

He pulled over, not knowing what was going on. The young men did not look familiar, so he felt something fishy was up.

Two men came out of his trap with a duffle bag.

"Fuck!" he yelled, knowing his spot was just robbed.

Big Choppa had a pistol in his truck, but he wasn't dumb. He knew if he went against them, he would die so he sat there.

Looking hard at the two men, he saw Tae's face, and he remembered him from the fair last week.

Big Choppa's blood boiled. He called Big Zone to tell him what was going on before his eyes.

This was his first time being robbed, and he felt like a bitch. Even though deep down he was a big pussy, he had an image to withhold in the streets.

Chapter 17
Durham, N.C.

Stacy had her legs spread wide as Scrilla's cock fit easily inside her lubed up slit as she relaxed, letting him invade her hole.

"Uhmmm shit, Scrilla," Stacy moaned and grew more aroused. She loved the way Scrilla took his time to make love to her.

The hotel's mattress rocked back and forth.

"I can take more," she said as her tiny little pussy managed to accommodate the whole thing.

Scrilla went deeper, making his rod disappear inside of her, and then emerge glistening with her juices.

"Yesss!" she screamed while he rammed in and out with a few hard thrusts, making her cum in a rapid-fire series of spasms.

"I need a break," Scrilla said as he sat up, slightly out of breath.

"You need a break?" she asked, getting out of the bed showing her slim petite ass.

Scrilla knew Stacy had to go back to her boyfriend, and he had shit to do also, so a little quickie was perfect.

He had to admit as he watched Stacy get dressed that she was a bad bitch with some good pussy. Stacy had that type of wetty that would make a nigga go crazy, so he knew whoever her man was, she had him hooked.

They had been kicking it for a while now, and they only called each other when they both wanted sex.

"I see you getting a little money," she said, looking at the Givenchy outfit and his new chain he was rocking.

"Nah."

"Whatever, handsome," she said, kissing him on the lips.

"I'ma hit you up next week," Scrilla said, seeing Main calling him.

"Ok, be safe," she said, sneaking out of the room as if someone was watching her.

Scrilla laughed because he knew how trifling bitches were these days.

***

Spelman College, ATL

Olivia was in her room doing some homework on her laptop for her criminal justice major she was taking. At twenty, she had her life in order, unlike her brother Scrilla.

She chose to come to school in Atlanta to get away from Durham because it was getting crazy out there.

Olivia was a beautiful young woman honey complexioned, long brown hair she dyed, chink eyes, thick, and the only flaw she disliked about herself was her teeth. For years, she had braces.

Coming to college was the best thing she ever did in her life. She knew as a black woman, it was hard to succeed in life without an education.

Her school was an all girl's school, so it was crazy. There were a lot of lesbians there trying to turn out all the young innocent women.

Olivia's roommate was a bi-sexual chick from Texas. She was cool. Olivia knew she liked her, but she didn't get down like that at all.

She was getting tired from hours of reading and studying. She was supposed to go out to have a drink today with a few girls from her school, but she couldn't.

Her roommate was a party girl, but she wasn't at all. Olivia was focused on how to make a make-up App for women to buy make-up at a low price.

Olivia was a born hustler by heart. Her family were go-getters. There were a few chicks from Durham there, but they were mostly white chicks.

***

Raleigh, N.C.

Big Choppa pulled up to a section called Lil Mexico in the southeast area of the city.

He parked near a school earlier in the morning to see Big Zone sitting and reading a newspaper.

"Big homie, what up?" Big Choppa said as he pulled up on his plug.

"What happened?" Big Zone asked, already knowing Big Choppa didn't call him for no reason.

"We got a problem," Big Choppa said, a little nervous.

"We? Choppa, where the fuck is my money," Big Zone said, putting the paper down.

One thing everybody knew was Big Zone didn't play when it came to his money. He would go ham.

"I got robbed."

"You got what?" Big Zone asked, hoping his ears heard him wrong.

"Some little niggas robbed me." Big Choppa was ashamed to even say he got robbed.

"Who are they?"

"One of them niggas is Justin. He's a Blood," Big Choppa said.

"Ok." Big Zone got up and walked off, as Big Choppa followed.

"What do you want me to do?" Big Choppa asked, seeing Big Zone step.

"Do you have my money?" Big Zone asked, looking at Big Choppa's puppy dog eyes.

"No."

Big Zone pulled out his gun and aimed it at Big Choppa's face.

"Please, bruh!" Big Choppa cried out.

Boc...

Boc...

Boc...

Boc...

"Bitch ass nigga." Big Zone spit on his little cousin, walking off.

Big Zone walked down the street to his car, thinking who was Justin and if they were the little niggas he been hearing about.

He knew his cousin would be a weak dot in his circle, so he had to get rid of him, and he let him know and see too much.

Big Zone was tying all loose ends just so he wouldn't have the fumbles that most hustlers have.

Chapter 18
Weight County, N.C.

Hustle had a few homes, but his main place was his 20,421 square foot mansion he had built ground up. Normally, his daughter would be there, but she was on her birthday vacation in Miami with her friends.

His mansion estate provided seamless indoor-outdoor living thanks to several patios. They had a big backyard and a kitchen that was attached to a bar out back. There was also a detached pool house that his daughter basically lived in.

The mansion had six bedrooms and four and a half bathrooms. Also, there was a five-car garage in the front area that he used for his luxury cars.

In a few hours, he had a meeting with a business man to go over some blueprints for a restaurant he wanted to open up in Rocky Mountain.

After his meeting, he would have to prepare some product for his crew because they were getting dry. For some reason, he had been feeling like someone had been watching him, so he had been moving slowly and not getting his hands dirty.

Hustle knew the feds had been trying to get him for a long time, but he was too smart. He planned them at their own game.

**

Durham, N.C.

M.I. had a house on Gray Street where he used to let women sell pussy out of it, and he took most of the profit.

Ten chicks were running on phones setting up dates with their Johns for the night.

He didn't like calling himself a pimp, he considered himself a Mack the way he handled his women.

Coming from a line of pimps, he knew he would sooner or later follow the footsteps of his dad.

M.I.'s father was a pimp, so he used to watch him growing up. YN was on his way. M.I. walked outside to see YN's hooked up Chevy rolling up the street on 26-inch rims, looking clean.

M.I. had to go across in a few, he just stopped by to check on his profits and making sure his main bitch was doing her job.

"You on sumthin?" YN asked, pulling up to the crib.

"Nah, I need a ride to The Bricks," M.I. said.

"Hop in."

"You riding dirty, my nigga?" M.I. knew how his young boy rolled Draco's and AK's all in the trunk and seat.

"Nah, bruh. That shit all in the stash spot. You feel me?" YN pushed the passenger door open for him.

M.I. hoped in taking a deep breath hoping they ain't get pulled over. Most of the police knew who he was and what he was into.

"What's going on? I ain't heard from you since you got the weight," M.I. said.

"To be honest, I be focused on trying to run up this bag and keep tabs on this Scrilla, and I'm starting to think somebody is sending him at us," YN said.

"At us?"

"Yeah, because they robbing our main people, our main source of income. These niggas killed City's mama crying out loud," YN stated driving down the busy street.

"You said you know where the little nigga be at, right?" M.I. asked.

"Yeah."

"Iight. Slide on him and make it count. What else is there to say, youngin?" M.I. told him.

"I'ma handle it."

"I know you will, but you heard from Clinton?" M.I. asked about his little cousin who was getting money on the Southside.

"Clinton doing numbers in the CW," said YN.

"When you get time check on him because his mom called me today and said she knows something is wrong because his phone is off, and he haven't been home to his baby mother's crib," M.I. said worried about his little cousin.

"I gotta go over there anyway," YN stated, making a left turn into the projects they called The Bricks.

"Good." M.I. got out and everybody was showing him love.

YN pulled off on his way to see if Clinton was ok because YN liked Clinton. He was a young, solid dude.

***

Durham, N.C.

In a lower basement somewhere in Da Mack, which was a dangerous projects only few could enter.

"Where is the fucking money, hoe ass nigga!" Main yelled about to crack Clinton's knee cap again.

A gang of Crips surrounded Clinton as they took turns on beating him for days now in the basement since they kidnapped him.

Main heard Clinton was getting big-time paper, and he wanted a piece.

"M.I.'s gonna kill all ya'll fuck niggas!" Clinton yelled, spitting out blood and teeth on the cold cement floor.

"Fuck M.I. Now where is the rest of the shit?" Main said because they only got 50,000 from him, which was a good hit, but he knew if he had fifty thousand he had more in the cut.

"Get it in, Blood bitch," Clinton said, acting tough.

"You sure?"

"You heard me, bruh."

"'Iight." Main laughed out loud with an evil laugh.

Bloc...

Bloc...

Bloc...

Bloc...

"Put his body in the trunk of Phil's car and drop him off where we found him. I'ma go get up with Scrilla." Main walked off wondering how he knew M.I.

Romell Tukes

Chapter 19
Southeast Raleigh

Tae rode around in his new car, a smoke gray Hellcat Widebody, which had a very powerful punch in the gas that made the engine roar up and down the streets.

On his left, he saw a gas station. He pulled over to get some gas real quick before sliding out to Rocky Mountain to see his sister Bri.

The relationship with his sisters was something he knew he should work on because he had been realizing it lately.

He knew Bri was on her independent shit, but he could hear it in her voice that she needed help, so he was making it his issue to drop her off some money.

When Bri told him she was working at a bar, he got upset because he believed she could start doing something better with herself.

Tae had been saving and spending money daily, but his uncle was putting him in a good position by setting up licks. Tae remembered everything his cousin Low Dee said about his uncle, but Tae already could tell Will was a snake.

Tae believed any nigga who would line up this many drug dealers, even ones they knew and fucked with, had to have some type of venom in their heart.

Pulling into the gas area, he saw a familiar face get out and walk in the store with a phat ass.

Tae had been so busy he hadn't had any time for chicks except the one he'd been texting back and forth with named Rena.

Getting to know Rena was cool. Not only was she smart, but she was one of the baddest chicks he ever met in person.

Walking into the store to pay for his gas, he got a closer look at the woman's face to see it was Winny.

He and Winny went to school together, and they had a good close bond, but he hadn't seen her in years.

The last he heard about Winny was she went off to the army and lost a leg and arm, but looking at her, the only thing different he saw was her phat ass.

In school, Winny used to be a skinny nerdy chick with a cute face nobody wanted to talk to because she had braces.

"Winny?" Tae said.

"Tae! Oh my God. Whatssss up? I was just talking about you the other day with somebody," Winny said, giving him a light hug.

"You look good," he said, looking at her small waist and curves.

"Boy, stop." She laughed.

"Nah, shawty. You look good." Tae saw how phat her camel toe print was and couldn't help but stare. Winny saw him looking and blushed.

"Tae, you a bad boy. I gotta stay away from you," Winny stated as Tae paid for his gas and followed her.

"I heard you went to the army and got your leg blown off or some shit?" Tae asked, looking at her legs.

"No, don't believe everything you hear," she shot back.

"So, what happened?"

"I was in an AV, and we got hit. The shit blew up. I lost two friends that day, but I didn't lose any body parts," Winny said, trying not to think of her recent experience overseas in Iraq.

"Damn."

"Yeap, but what you got going on out here? I've been hearing you and Justin stay in some shit out here."

"Don't believe everything you hear," Tae told her using her shit.

Winny was a redbone cutie with a big butt and big round eyes, but the only problem was her height. She stood close to six feet, but her sex appeal was so strong to the opposite sex that her height didn't matter to most males.

"So, what are you doing with yourself? You got a nice car, nice clothes, and you looking like money. I just hope it's from the right choices in life," she said.

"You finna judge me like everybody else?"

"I'm not everybody else, Tae. I have brothers who do the same shit, and it's not cool. You're playing with your life," she warned him, pumping gas in her Lexus sedan.

"I'm good. When you free, maybe we can link up?" he asked.

"I don't know."

"Know about what?"

"Tae, you live a crazy life. I been hearing about you. I don't want to put myself in no situation."

"I don't know what you heard, but I'm not doing no crazy shit outchea."

"Whatever, but I don't like giving out my number," she told him.

"Ok."

"Hit me in the DM and don't send no dick pics." She giggled.

"Wouldn't you like to be lucky," he joked back, filling up his car.

"Bye, Tae."

"Bye, phat butt," Tae replied as she gave him the evil eye.

Tae drove 30 minutes up to Rocky Mountain to see Bri.

***

North, Durham

Peach was the whore house's main hoe. She was the one who set up dates, collected payments from customers, kept track of how many hoes were working, and hired and fired new young ladies.

Today four ladies were working, but it was a dead Sunday, so all the chicks were in the living room doing each other's nails and hair.

Peach used to be M.I.'s main hoe before he started selling drugs and got rich, but when she got fat due to her depression and three miscarriages by him, he found another job for her, which was her current position.

He made so much money off Peach selling pussy and sucking dick. He knew fucking her was the wrong thing to do because that would cause an emotional attachment.

One thing M.I. knew about the pimp game was to never have a sexual or emotional attachment to your whores, or they will eventually disobey your authority.

Pimping was a ninety percent mind thing. M.I. tried to show Peach the same game, and she soaked it up.

"Ya'll bitches need to get ya'll stank asses in the shower. I'ma have two guests later, so get that ass and pussy together!" Peach yelled, smoking a blunt coming downstairs.

"I'm on my period," a skinny dark-skinned chick said with big lips and a huge gap between her teeth.

"Well, I'm sure you can suck some dick. I heard your head game is the best in here," Peach stated.

"Yes, it is," she replied, knowing she would be doing a lot of blow jobs for the next few days.

"Good now -"

BOOM!

The front door flew open, and three gunmen entered with weapons

Tat... Tat... Tat... Tat... Tat... Tat... Tat... Tat...

Scrilla and his goons shot all the hookers except Peach, who didn't know what to do.

"Where is M.I.?"

"Who?" Peach's voice got dry.

"M.I. bitch, don't fucking play wit me. I'll blow your shit off," Scrilla said, placing his gun to her forehead.

"He only comes here on Friday to collect the dues," Peach cried.

"Iight. Well, tell him Scrilla looking for him and where is that money?"

"Right there in the drawer." Peach pointed next to the mini bar she had installed.

One of Scrilla's goons went to get the cash the women had been fucking and sucking for.

"Take care, big girl." Scrilla slapped her on her phat ass and left.

Peach couldn't deny the fact that Scrilla had her pussy wet. She was gonna tell M.I. everything, but she started to wonder who the man was.

She was snapped out of her trance when she saw the dead bodies in the living room. She called the police then M.I.

Romell Tukes

Chapter 20
Rocky Mountain

Bri and Tae were chilling at her apartment, drinking and talking.

"What's up wit mommy?"

"I barely see her nowadays, but you know how she do," Tae said, sitting on her couch flipping through the TV trying to find something to watch.

"Yeah, what you been up to? I see you dressed fly as shit," she stated.

"Chilling, dawg. Trying to get to it."

"You got a new car. You doing good," she stated, sitting down with a bowl of chicken she made earlier.

"I'm starting to make moves."

"You selling drugs because if so, I need some," she said nonchalantly.

"What?!! You doing drugs now?" Tae couldn't believe his ears at all. He would've never pictured his sister doing drugs.

"Nah, at my job it be mad money up in there. I can make a killing in that bitch, bruh."

"Oh, yeah." Tae saw dollar signs, but the only issue was he didn't want to put his sister's life in danger.

"I don't want you selling that shit cause you could easily get knocked off and be stuck in some jail cell, and you got a lot going on. You got a crib, car, and bills."

"Tae, I know how to move. I'm not green, and I know a few chicks willing to sell that shit," Bri said.

"Oh, well. I'ma see what I can do," Tae said.

"'Iight, but I'm serious."

"For sho. I got you, sis."

"You better. I'm trying to get money," Bri told him.

"Have patience and trust me," Tae told her while watching TV.

***

Durham, N.C.

Main was going to pick up his little sister from high school and take her out to eat. Lately, he hadn't been spending time with her because he had been running the streets.

Word already hit the streets that Main and Scrilla were on straight bullshit. Scrilla recently ran up in M. I.'s hoe house and killed a few of his hoes. Main found that pointless, but let Scrilla do him.

700 Block niggas were getting money now. Even the little niggas were running around trying to sell weed and pills.

Main cruised down the street seeing a few people stare at the tinted windows to his left. Then out of nowhere, he heard gunfire coming from the side of the car.

Boc...

Boc...

Boc...

Boc...

Boc...

Main ducked and hit a young man about to cross the street on a bicycle knocking him off.

Main went 60 mph and sped up trying to get the fuck away from the trap they set him up in.

"Bitch ass niggas," Main said to himself looking at the sunlight shine through the bullet holes that entered the seats.

Main went up a few blocks and made it to his sister's school in a few minutes.

His little sister was out front with a few of her friends when she saw her brother's car pull up with bullet holes.

Main's little sister was Betty. She was 16 and a little pretty chick and very smart in school. She had one year left. She was so smart the teachers skipped her a grade up.

"Damn, Main. What the fuck happened?" she asked, opening the door.

"Just get in."

"What is going on?"

"What does it look like?" Main was always real with Betty.

"Who is dumb enough to shoot up a car in broad daylight?"

"You'd be surprised," he stated.

"People are so dumb, but what's up? How was your day since dropping me off?" Betty asked, staring at the bullet holes and being funny.

"You got jokes."

"I'm starving."

"I'ma go get you something to eat after I get a new car."

"New car?" she replied back, seeing nothing wrong with the car except the bullet holes.

"Facts."

"Get me one."

"Graduate."

"Ok, deal." Betty knew he wouldn't lie to her, so she was geeked.

***

Greensboro, N.C.

Spin had some family in Greensboro in a hood called High Point. He had a few cousins out there, and it was the city of the big college football events. Everybody came out to the college events. It was like the super bowl of the city.

Since killing the cop, he'd been laying low in Greensboro just in case any cops got wind of any footage of him doing it, but he was on a bike, so he figured he was good.

Will and Banks told him to come back in a week. He was going back to his hood.

His cousin Nay was in Atlanta getting money, but his other cousin Rocy was in the next room fucking a fat bitch.

The fat chick wanted him to fuck next, but Spin just wanted the neck. Shawty was 300 plus and he hated leftovers.

Rocy was getting a little money in High Point, but Spin was about to put him on to some real money.

The dope money in High Point was crazy. If Rocy had the right plug, he could make up to 100,000 every other day if he was focused.

Spin and Rocy had planned to hit up a club and have fun, but he was in the room making love to a fat bitch.

"Hurry up!" Spin yelled through the door.

"Nigga, hold up!" Rocy yelled back holding his moans because the chick's head game was crazy. Her head was wet, slippery, and she deep throated at the same time.

Chapter 21
Raleigh, N.C.

Tae was driving to a four-star restaurant called Hibachi 88, which was known for its good food. Today, Tae had a date night with Rena. She finally gave in to letting him take her out to dinner.

He felt a little nervous because he felt like Rena was a classy young chick who had her head on straight, unlike most women he ran into.

Rena was supposed to meet him there any minute, so he parked in the front and fixed himself up. He had on a nice Dior outfit with a fresh smelling cologne.

Once inside the restaurant, he took a good look around before a waitress approached him. After he was seated at a table, he asked the waitress to bring their best wine. Earlier, he called and informed the restaurant that he would arrive at that time.

He was brought to a nice table for two that had a white cloth and candles on top of it.

Seconds later, Rena came walking inside wearing a silk Miu Miu dress with heels. Tae had to do a double take because he didn't know the slim woman was holding the way she was.

Rena's curves and breasts stood out the most. She was looking sexy tonight and Tae knew he had to come right because there may not be a second time.

"Hey, Tae." She smiled with her flirtatious eyes.

"Thanks for coming. Let me pull that seat out for you, beautiful." Tae pulled out her chair, taking a sneak peek at her phat round perfectly shaped ass. Rena had a curvy hourglass shape from her hitting the gym at least four days a week.

"I wouldn't miss this day if I had to. You been telling me everything I wanna hear on the phone, so I couldn't wait to see you face to face," she said.

"I'm here. I'm willing to open up and be honest with you."

"Honest, huh?" She smirked.

"How many brothers you know can say that?" he joked.

"None, but I got a question. How many hoes you got because I don't need a chick trying to kill me," she said, seeing many situations like that.

"I'm single because I'm focused on my life and I'ma need a chick I can trust and depend on."

"Like a ride or die type bitch," she added.

"Yeah, because I live a crazy lifestyle."

"Well, I guess it's pointless to ask you what you do for a living." She knew his type, but she didn't judge him.

There were times she would call, and he would have to gang up, go somewhere, or there would be a lot of people around him.

"What's understood ain't gotta be said."

"I feel that, but what do you look for in women?" she wanted to know.

"You."

"Me? What about me?" Rena didn't like his fast reply.

"Well you're sexy, smart, a paralegal, kind, open-minded and you classy wit a dab of ratchet in you." He made her laugh so hard her water almost spilled out of her mouth.

"You crazy," she said, about to order their food.

Rena was a paralegal and hoped to become a lawyer within a year or two.

The date went smooth and great. They didn't want to end it, but they both had to get home.

***

North Raleigh, N.C.

Club Touchdown was a spot Justin had been to only twice, and he wished he would've started coming out there more because the place was turned up to the max tonight.

He brought out a gang of his little niggas to party and have a good time.

There was so much beef going on in the city. Justin needed a night to relax and loosen up. Something he never had time to do now.

Hearing about Big Choppa's death, he had a feeling that it was Big Zone's work because of the robbery. The robbery came in handy for the crew. They were up locking shit down, but Justin's main worry was if his boy Tae would be able to stay constantly.

An hour later, Justin was ready to slide to another club called Diva's just to enjoy his night.

He was trying to call Tae, so he could come out to have a good time, but the call went to voicemail.

Outside, Justin saw two trucks pull up as he was about to cross the street leading into the parking lot.

***

"Big Zone, who them?" one of Big Zone's soldiers asked, seeing a gang cross the street passing their trucks.

"That's them little niggas. Get them, fool!" Big Zone shouted as his men jumped out with their guns cocked.

Boc…

Boc…

Boc…

Boc…

Boc…

Boc…

Bullets struck one of Justin's friends in the back, and his goon reacted with fire.

Justin saw Big Zone with the gunmen before he ducked low on the side of a Benz truck that belonged to someone in his crew.

Bloc… Bloc… Bloc… Bloc…

Bloc… Bloc… Bloc… Bloc…

Justin hit one of the gunmen in the leg, but three seconds later, his cousin caught two bullets to the head, dropping him in front of him.

Gunfire continued to erupt for a few more seconds,and then police sirens were heard and everybody scattered.

Jason hurt seeing two of his people laying in their blood as he got in his car. His crew all got in their whips, racing off.

Chapter 22
Downtown, Raleigh

Rena sat in a law firm office looking at the flowers she just received from Tae moments ago, and they smelled and looked good.

She loved white roses and had expressed that to Tae days ago. This confirmed that he listened to her, and she really liked that about him.

Her last boyfriend ended up moving to LA to become an actor, and she never saw him again or heard from him.

Being in love and falling in love was something she was trying to stay away from, but there was something about Tae that made her want to love again.

Living a single free life was cool but at times, she would be horny and get lonely wishing she had someone to cuddle with.

Rena had a lunch date with her father in half an hour on her lunch break, so she was about to leave.

Rena and her dad were real close. They had more of a brother and sister bond, which was cool.

Rena's mom was never in the picture. She moved to New York when she was a baby and never came back.

Her dad did a great job at raising Rena, and she had a lot of respect for him because of that alone.

Checking the time, she knew it was time to go, so she got her IPhone and purse, leaving the office. She wore a nice business suit.

***

Southeast, Raleigh

Will was in the back seat of the Maybach while Bank drove to a section called NBA.

"I had a little chick almost get caught up in that crossfire last night," Bank said.

"What crossfire?" Will had no clue of what Bank was talking about.

"At the new club called Touchdown. There was a shootout."

"I never been there, but how bad was it?"

"Three dead, but I'm hearing it was Tae's people. You feel me?" Bank said, driving slowly about to make a left.

It was a hot summer day and people were out fanning themselves down trying to beat the heat, but there was no running from 105 degree heat.

"Tae's doing good, but he don't know that this is the start of his small troubles." Will chuckled.

"What you got in mind next for him?"

"I don't know, but this Big Zone nigga is becoming a pain in my ass."

"Me, too. You want me and Spin to handle him?" Bank had no problem taking care of his boss' dirty work.

"Nah, let Tae deal with it. That's why I sent him his way."

"Ok."

"I got something else planned for you," Will said as the Maybach pulled over.

"Spin on his way back."

"You spoke to him?" Will asked, needing his young boy back.

"Yes, in a few days he told me," Bank said, getting out.

"Good. I'ma need him to handle this YN kid in Durham. I think I put too much on Scrilla."

"He got his 700 crew, right?" Bank walked with Will into a building.

"They can't handle M.I."

"You think he knows you're the one pushing all the buttons?" Banks asked.

"Maybe. He's a smart kid, just like his dad." Will thought back to M.I.'s dad, who was Will's best friend until they got into a situation over some money and Will snaked him.

Will robbed and killed M.I.'s dad in front of M.I.'s grandmom on some gangsta shit.

Little did Will know, M.I. saw Will leave after the gunshots woke him up out of his sleep.

Lasting long in the game, Will knew you had to become a snake point blank, so he lived by that mind frame.

Inside the building on the second level floor, he had an apartment where a few trustworthy people cooked up drugs for him to sell.

***

East Durham, N.C.

Scrilla was taking a chick to a local clinic, so she could get an abortion. When she came to him talking about he got her pregnant, he knew what needed to be done.

The lady rode in the passenger seat, upset because she wanted to have his baby and put him on child support just like her mom told her to. When she heard Scrilla was getting money, she put a hole in the condom four times.

At first, she refused to have an abortion until Scrilla threatened her life.

Scrilla stopped at the intersection of a busy street to see a door open up behind him and YN hopped out with a Draco airing out his car.

Tat... Tat... Tat... Tat... Tat... Tat... Tat... Tat...

Scrilla pulled off, seeing the girl's head slam into the dashboard, leaking from the headshot. Scrilla drove to the hospital to drop her off and kept pushing, but he was glad he could save 600 dollars on an abortion.

Romell Tukes

Chapter 23
Westside, Raleigh

Tae and Justin rode around trying to come up with a better plan to network and expand their drug trade.

"What you was saying about Rocky Mountain the other day, bro?" Justin asked as he rode through the ghetto.

"Nah, my sister was telling me how it's some money out there and shit."

"Who Bri?" Justin asked, already knowing, but he just wanted to hear it again. Since a little kid, he always had a crush on her and got nervous whenever he entered her presence.

"Yeah, fool," Tae shot back.

"So let's open up shop. I heard it's a lot of money up there."

"Me too, bro. So, I think I'ma send some of the little homies up there to give her a pack and see how it turns out," Tae added.

"Facts."

"I just don't want her to get in trouble or knocked with the shit. You feel me?" Tae knew Bri wasn't a drug dealer, so one slip up, and she could end up in somebody's cage and God forbid if she told.

"I think she good, bro. Bri know how to get money and how to move under pressure, dawg."

"True dat," Tae agreed with him on that.

Driving down Garmen Street, they saw a lot of traffic and movement going on in one of the houses.

Crackheads and dopefiends were lined up around the block, running in and out of the green and blue house.

It was close to noon in the middle of the month, so both men knew what was going on, someone was getting money.

"Pull over and park, bruh," Justin told Tae as they both thought the same thing.

"I got a better idea," Tae said. Justin pulled out a gun and knew what he wanted to do.

"What's that?" Justin asked, already focused on airing out the spot because he knew this was Big Zone and Lil B's side of town.

Lil B was a Blood kid who worked for Big Zone and a real shooter. He didn't play no games. Whenever a nigga came at Lil B, they had to come right.

"Yo, let me buy y'all hoodies and hats!" Tae yelled out of his window, seeing two crackheads speed walk by them.

Both of the fiends stopped when they heard the word buy.

"How much?" a fiend with no teeth asked, sucking on his gums.

"A hundred a piece," Tae replied, seeing their eyes light up.

Justin knew what he was getting at with this, and he laughed to himself.

The fiends rushed to take off the hoodies and hats.

"You want the shirt and draws, too? I'll give it to you for fifty," the other man said, seeing Tae peel off two blue faces off a big wad of money.

"Nah, dawgy. We cool wit dis," Justin added, putting on the dirty hat.

The crackheads pocketed the money and left, racing off to get back in line across the street to cop some more drugs from the trap.

"Dis shit smells like piss," Tae said while putting on the hoodie.

"This was your idea, bruh. I'm just following your lead." Justin held his breath while putting on the hoodie. It smelled so bad.

***

CR and Rex had been selling work for the last three hours. Fiends were running in and out of the trap since the doors opened up. The police barely fucked with them, even with lines of fiends flooding the block at times.

The men worked for Lil B, who was Big Zone's little nephew. They sold mostly dog food on that side of town and every morning from 6 to 11 it was rush hour because people needed their wake and bake.

"How much we got left?" Rex asked, holding the door down with a Draco, as CR screwed the dope fiends hand to hand.

This was the men's routine. CR would pitch the work and Rex would let them in two or three at a time while he looked out for robberies and police.

"I think a half of bird plus these eighty bundles, Blood," CR said, waiting for more dope heads to enter.

"Aight. Lil B texted me and said he will be here a little after one," Rex said, looking at his phone while two dope fiends walked inside.

"Don't move," a voice said, putting a gun to Rex's head while taking the Draco out of his hand.

Toe rushed up to CR and patted him down to only feel money.

"Who trap is this?" Tae asked CR.

"Lil B, bruh. You finna make a mistake," CR shot back, looking at the black bag full of money on the table from a day of hard work.

"Iight, thug. This all y'all got?" Tae asked, getting the money in the bag.

"Yeah, but it belongs to Lil B," said Rex before Justin blew his head off. Tae shot CR four times, then walked out to see dope fiends looking to see what happened. When they saw guns instead of running, they waited for Tae and Justin to leave before they raided the trap for drugs, not caring about the bodies.

Romell Tukes

Chapter 24
Durham, N.C.

Bank and Will had been tailing the black Chevy pickup truck for almost a whole day now, since Will had been feeling bad vibes from a man named Peter.

Will met Peter a few months ago. One of his side bitches introduced him to Peter. She told Will that Peter was getting big money in Greenville and Durham. When she told Will he needed a plug, Will felt Peter out, then he started to deal with him. Will always had Bank pass out drugs and collect money.

Twice he sold weight to Peter, but for some reason each time he felt as if Peter was a little nervous or scared. His side bitch spoke so highly of Peter, he took her word until she got ghost on Will.

What drove Will crazy thinking about the shit was when she ghosted him, so did Peter, and he had Bank track the man down, and he did just that.

Will had been following the man all day, and he didn't see nothing out of the ordinary about Peter. Besides, he moved low-key under the radar.

"This nigga weird," Bank said.

"He's different, but I ain't seen him do a drug transaction all day." Will watched the pickup truck closely as they kept a good distance.

"Either he's smooth or ran out of work." Bank was driving. He was focused on the road as they drove into a suburban area on the outskirts of Durham.

"If he was out of work, why not call me? This dude changed his number, Bank. I find that suspect."

"I feel that, bruh," Banks said, seeing the pickup truck pull into a driveway.

Bank parked down the street, shutting off the car headlights to see Peter got out with a bag and walked in the house as if he didn't have a care in the world.

Peter made a few steps to a store, and he met up with an older white man for a few seconds, and that was it.

"You got a plan?" Bank asked.

"No, just have my back and follow my lead, something ain't right," Will said, climbing out of the car.

Will knocked on the door and seconds later a thick cute white woman approached the door, opening it, looking at Bank and Will. She'd never seen them before.

"Hello, can I help you?" She was Peter's wife for ten years.

Will wasted no time and pulled out his gun, aiming it at her head as Bank followed suit.

"Baby! Who's that? The neighbors?" Peter yelled from the living area a few feet away. When he walked towards the front door, his wife had tears in her eyes, walking towards him with her hands in the air.

"What the fuck, Will?" Peter couldn't believe what was going on.

"Shut da fuck up and go sit down in the living room." Will turned Peter around, rushing him into the living room, grabbing the back of his neck.

"What the fuck is going on?" Peter and his wife were seated on the couch.

"Who the hell are you, Peter? Why I haven't heard from you?" Will asked looking at the pictures in the photo frames around the room.

"I lost my phone. I lost your number, man. I was going to come find you, bro. I promise," Peter said as his wife put her head down, shaking it in fear. She knew that both of their lives were in danger.

Peter was a tall, handsome, brown-skinned brother with a white woman as a wife. He acted and spoke like a white boy because he was raised by white foster parents, and he was the only black kid in his private school growing up.

Will saw something that caught his attention: a photo of Peter in a Marine uniform while overseas holding an assault rifle, then above that, he saw a paper that read Agent Michael Fields.

"You're a fucking cop!" Will said out loud. Peter's eyes widened as he looked at his name on the paper. What happened next was a dead giveaway.

"I told you not to take the fucking job. Now look! Jesus Christ! You're so dumb! After this, I want a divorce! I hate this marriage. I've stopped loving you. I want a divorce!" Peter's wife yelled out in tears, causing a confused look to cover Peter's face.

Bank stood there in shock, wondering why the FBI was on Will's line.

"You a fed," Will said as his mind continued to race.

"Yes, I'm a federal agent that was building a case on you. The chick who introduced us was a C.I. informant," Peter admitted. Whose real name was Michael. He used the name Peter to hide his real identity.

"What type of shit you got on me?" Will had a feeling someone was watching him.

"Not so much you because when I went in for the wiretaps and footage you sent him," Peter pointed at Bank.

"Oh, had on me?" Bank looked surprised, as if he just won a million dollar lotto.

"Yes, we did two drug deals and money transactions. That is enough to bring down a federal indictment," Peter told him.

"Fuck!" Bank yelled, feeling like Will set him up.

"So, you have nothing on me?" Will asked.

"No, just photos."

"Good, but I need you to get rid of his case and make it disappear," Will said.

"I can't. I'll have to steal the file."

"Until you get it done, her life and your life depends on it. We'll be taking her until it's over, and you handle your part." Will snatched Peter's wife by her hair, dragging her out of the crib.

Romell Tukes

Chapter 25
N.C. State University

Bri decided to enroll in college. It was something she planned to do a long time ago, but being flooded with bills and work, she had no time for school.

Now since she quit her job, she had been very busy hustling for Tae and getting herself in college like her sister who attended a college in Atlanta.

Bri wanted to take Business Management, so she could stack up enough money to open up her own businesses.

Tae had two of his sliders from her old hood in Raleigh she used to see outside being bad now transporting drugs.

The first time she saw coke, she didn't know what to do with it. The young niggas bagged everything up for her at her crib.

She knew a lot of coke heads from her job that had been buying the drugs up. She had less than two hundred grams of coke to sell. Bri never saw so much money in her life. She now knew why it was hard for niggas to stop selling drugs when they were making so much money.

Walking through the campus, she saw everybody enjoying the college, seeing students chilling in the grass having a picnic and doing some studying.

Bri already filled out her app online, so her first class started today. She was excited about it.

She was looking like a schoolgirl in uniform, heels, and designer shades. She was looking like a snack.

***

Myrtle Beach, S.C.

Tae and Rena went out on the beach to enjoy a day together and spend some time getting to know each other.

Rena couldn't believe how many people were out enjoying the hot nice day outside. She laid on her stomach on the beach getting a tan.

"I never been out here," Rena said.

"Me either."

"What made you want to come out here?" she asked.

"I wanted to see you in a bikini to be honest," he said, looking at the bikini stuck in her perfectly shaped ass.

"Boy, stop playing." She hit him on his arm as they looked at the beach water.

"I really like spending time with you, sexy."

"Oh, is that right?" Rena blushed.

"Facts." Tae rubbed her shoulders.

"Oh, so big facts." Rena laughed at Tae's sense of humor.

"I really want you," Tae said as she looked at him in his eyes to see if he was honest.

Rena had been feeling the same way, but she had been scared to approach the situation out of fear of denial.

"Tae, stop playing."

"Nah, I'm serious. Since I met you, I haven't been able to get you out my mind. Facts. And, you're everything I want in a woman." Tae saw how big her smile was.

"I feel the same way, Tae."

"So, you babe now?" he asked.

"Big facts period…" she said, laughing. They shared their first kiss.

***

Downtown Durham

M.I. took his time rolling his blunt as he leaned on his car outside of the flea market waiting for his grandmom to come out.

M.I.'s g-mom loved shopping at flea markets every weekend and just his luck, he was her personal driver every Saturday morning. Since a few of his hoes were killed in his whore house, he'd been upset about that and hunting down Scrilla.

His bottom whore told him the man who raided the house was named Scrilla. Even though pimpin was his side hustle, he still took it very serious, and he felt disrespected.

YN was waiting for him across town with the goons ready to slide down The 700 Block to see who was out.

Seeing his g-mom come out, he stopped rolling his blunt.

"Boy, if you don't come help me with these bags," his grandmom said slowly, making her way to him with a cart full of bags.

"My bad," he said, tucking his blunt because his grandmom hated the smell of weed. M.I. helped her load up the bags into his car and trunk.

***

Main and two of his boys were out early to grab a bite to eat from a fast food spot because they were starving from the long night out trapping.

Looking out of the window of the passenger seat, he saw M.I. loading bags into a Benz.

"Pull over, dawg. There go that nigga right there," Main said, pulling out his Glock 27 with a 30 shot clip attached to it.

The car pulled into the flea market lot and Main jumped out with the car still moving like a scene from an action movie.

Bloc...

Bloc...

Bloc...

Bloc...

Two of Main's bullets struck M.I.'s grandmom in the chest, knocking her off her feet.

M.I. saw this and grabbed the choppa he had in the open trunk.

Tat, Tat, Tat, Tat, Tat, Tat, Tat, Tat...

The rounds from the AK-47 landed directly into Main's shooters upper torsos. Main was down low trying to avoid being hit by one of the 223 bullets.

Main fired a few more shots at M.I. then saw his two goons bodies were numb, so before he became victim three he got in the car racing out of the lot knowing he wasn't ready for the AK vs his Glock.

Driving off, he saw M.I. trying to save the old woman lying on the ground in a pool of blood. Main didn't like shooting women, but she got caught in the crossfire, and when it's war nothing matters.

Chapter 26
Atlanta, GA

Olivia stepped outside of her car looking sexy in a pair of heels and a mini dress showing a lot of skin. She took a deep breath, looking at the club sign that read Blue Flame.

Olivia had been working there for a full month now, and she hated it, but this was her only way to see some real paper. She still attended college, but she needed fast money.

One of the girls she knew who lived in the dorm with her named Dream Baby gave Olivia the idea after telling Olivia how she could make some big money.

When Olivia heard 'big money' she wanted to know more, plus seeing Dream Baby drive a new BMW 8 series and wear a bunch of designer shit to class every day made her wonder.

Dream Baby told her how. She worked at the city strips at night time and was making nothing less than five bands a night just to dance, twerk, and slide up and down on a metal pole.

Everybody thought Olivia got her body done. Her ass was so fat with no stomach. Even Dream Baby asked her how much she paid for her ass and titties but when Olivia told her it was all real Dream couldn't believe it.

Dream Baby was only 20 years old and got her whole body done twice in Miami and DR.

She was working in strip clubs to make a little money because she had no financial support while down in college in Atlanta. All of Dream's family was back home in Brooklyn, NY, where she grew up.

Olivia would come four days out of the week and do her thing, then leave like a bat out of hell. One night she made eight bandz, but she was highly requested from the clients. They loved when she hit the stage.

Her stage name was Golden because of her golden-honey complexion.

She walked into the club and heard the loud rap music from an artist named NBA YoungBoy who was killing the club music at

Blue Flame. The club was packed as she walked through the crowd, seeing clients wave her down for a dance, but she had to get dressed.

Olivia saw women in private sections of the club bent over getting fucked doggy style with no shame.

Walking to the back dressing room, she saw a Spanish chick in the cut on her knees sucking a nigga's dick at a fast pace.

That's one thing she swore to never do, and that was to fuck or suck a nigga's dick in the club. Olivia felt that was to downgrade women, and she wasn't getting down like that.

Dream Baby told her she did private shows for niggas every night because that was where the real money was. One day, she remembered that Dream told her four niggas were taking turns fucking her in a hotel, and she got paid ten stacks for it.

In the dressing room, Olivia almost had to hold her nose. The musk smell was so strong.

When the dancers worked up a sweat all night dancing and doing pole tricks in a humid club, sooner or later Olivia knew a smell would soon linger.

Olivia placed her clothes in a locker, and she got dressed in a see-through gown, giving the public a view of her phat pussy and large areolas.

"Hey, Golden!" Two dancers said, coming in with bottles of Ace that they got from drunk customers who couldn't drink any more.

"Ya'll saw Dream?" Olivia asked, applying a little bit of eye shadow.

"She was behind us, but I think she made a quick stop in the bathroom to fuck some big dick nigga from Zone 3," Viral told her before walking off.

One thing Olivia realized early in the club was everybody knew everybody's business. To make shit worse, bitches in the club loved to count each other's money.

"Olivia ..." Dream yelled, walking in the room with a slight limp.

"Hey, bitch. Where you been and why you walking like that?" Olivia asked.

"Girl, this crazy nigga just tried to fuck me with a horse dick. That shit was like 14 inches."

"What? No way," Olivia said because she never saw nothing past a nine inch and her pussy was extra tight, so that was too much for her.

"Hell, yeah. As soon as he put it in, my walls almost ripped open. I had to stop him. I just gave him some head and that nigga came in five seconds. All that big shit for nothing." Dream Baby laughed thinking about how she put her twist game down on the dick. She knew all the tricks to make a nigga cum in seconds.

"You is crazy, but I gotta hit the stage," Olivia said, thinking about what song she should put on to work the stage and the crowd.

"I'ma hit it with you."

"No kissing me this time."

"Bitch, you got lucky that day," Dream said.

"Whatever, let's go." Olivia got up looking at her phat ass poking out in her gown.

Olivia told the club DJ to put on some Silk the song "Freak-Me" and she did her thing on the pole. Olivia did splits across the stage then to end it off her and Dream played in each other's pussy in front of the people hearing them moan as the gushy sounds could be heard over the music.

Olivia did a few private dances and left with 6,700 in one night, while Dream went off to an after party to paper chase.

Romell Tukes

Chapter 27
Downtown, Raleigh

The federal building was off New Bern Avenue right in the middle of the hood where it went down, and a nigga didn't give a fuck about a fed building being right in the middle of a hood.

Agent Moore sat in his booth wondering what he was going to do so he could get his wife back home safely. He knew what needed to be done, but it wasn't easy getting an active file. An active file was an open case that was being investigated and watched at the same time.

"Agent," a big white federal agent who looked like the actor The Rock said.

"What's going on, L." Moore called him by his nickname while taking his eyes off his wife's photo on his desk in his small office.

"You been out of it lately," L said, sitting down in an empty chair.

"Me?"

"Yeah, you. I hope everything is good?" L said, wondering if he knew about his secret affair with Moore's wife.

L really wanted to ask Moore why his wife wasn't anywhere around because he had been calling her. L had to admit Moore's wife had the best head he ever had in his life, but she was fucking and sucking half the federal building.

"I'm okay, just dealing wit some issues." Moore didn't want to get into it deep.

"You know you can talk to me, man."

"I know."

"How's the family?" L gave him a funny look to see if Moore was going to spill the beans about where his wife had been.

"Good."

"You sure?" L repeated.

"Yes, L."

"Ok, I'ma get back to work. Come out with me sometimes, and have a drink with me to release that stress." L stood up, thinking he must have caught his wife cheating or something.

"I will L." Moore got on his computer to act like he had work to do, but in reality he hadn't done any work since his wife had been kidnapped.

He had to find a way to sneak into his boss' office who was a workaholic, and the only time he wasn't rocking was on Sundays to attend church.

Moore had been plotting on how he was going to sneak into his office to steal the file, so he could get his wife back.

Then the next problem would be hacking into his boss' computer to delete whatever file they had on Bank and Will on the central files.

"Hey, Moore. I'ma go run out to the county jail real quick. I got a fucker who has been down there requesting me, for two weeks now," Moore's boss said rushing out of the office leaving his office door open.

"Ok, bossman!" Moore shouted, looking around to see the office was half empty.

Moore looked around, and he knew it was now or never to make his move. Getting into his boss' office would have been the hardest part, but he knew this was the perfect opportunity because the door was left open.

Moore got up, looking around to see the four or five people in the office busy on the phone or talking to each other. He got up smoothly and walked into his boss' office, which was only a few feet away from his office.

Once inside, Moore rushed for the file cabinets, looking for the Bank file which consisted of Will's also, but mainly everything involved Bank's dealings.

Moore looked through each drawer to find nothing in the first file cabinet. Then he made his way to the other file cabinet near the window.

The third file had Bank's folder in it. It was thick and red.

"Yes ..." Moore said, looking out of the office to make sure the coast was still clear because he knew if he got caught it would be over for his career. He could even go to jail.

The big problem was now because Moore didn't know his boss' password, and this was a big problem.

Moore touched the mouse key and the computer's screen turned on, but what popped up shocked him.

There was a sex video of two young little girls, both black having sex with an old white man. The man looked like his boss.

The young girls looked no older than ten years old. Moore was disgusted to the point he almost vomited all over the computer.

Moore logged out of the sex scene, went to the central files, and punched in the docket number on the folder.

When Bank's case came up on the computer, Moore deleted everything and quickly logged out, hearing his boss' voice in the building somewhere.

Moore placed the nasty sex video back on the computer and turned off the screen. He rushed back to his office just in time.

He placed the folder in his gym bag out of breath logging on to his computer as if he was busy working.

"Damn, Moore. I forgot something," his boss said, running into the office

"I know the feeling," Moore replied as he watched his boss go into the office and go straight to his computer.

Moore knew his boss must have been trying to exit out of the sex video he had with the minors. He watched his boss look around nervously, as if someone was watching him or caught him.

Seconds later, his boss came back out, looking around.

"I'm leaving, Moore. I'll see you later." His boss left again.

"Freak bitch," Moore mumbled under his breath.

"You say something?"

"Huh?"

"I thought you said something." His boss stepped out of his office door.

"No, have a good night."

"I will." His boss gave a big awkward look before leaving the office.

Moore prepared to leave. He did his part. Now he wanted to get his wife back.

***

Raleigh, N.C.

Bank had Agent Moore's wife on the outskirts of the city. She was in a safe house, cuffed up in a bedroom where she could watch TV and move around with his help.

Bank's soldiers ran around to do his little errands and get anything him or her needed.

Will came by last night and was supposed to be on his way over again to tell him something important.

Babysitting wasn't his thing at all. He needed more weed and liquor to get him through the days. Two nights ago, the woman asked him if they were going to kill her, and she would do anything to save her life. Then she went on to say how she loved black men and could make any man nut in seconds.

Hearing her say that Bank wanted to test the water, but he disliked white women with a passion.

She was asleep on the bed in panties, and Bank couldn't resist looking at her phat pussy poking out the panties. He had to take another look before walking out of the room to wait on Will. He just wanted to kill the bitch and get it over with, so he could continue on with his regular life hustling and getting to a bag.

Chapter 28
Raleigh, N.C.

Will was on his way to tell Bank the good news about how Agent Moore called him informing him that he had the file and everything was taken care of.

Will didn't really care about the feds building a case on Bank, but when he found out about his name being mentioned, he knew he had to do something quick.

With so much shit on his mind, he figured he'd call one of his brothers back who lived in Atlanta named Buzz. He was a getting money nigga also.

Last night, Will heard Hustle had been putting money on his head and that scared Will because he knew Hustle would do anything to get at him not only for Chess's death, but Will was slowly but surely taking out Hustle's crew.

Talking to one of his young boys, he heard Hustle had a bad daughter who was a lawyer, and he planned to holla at Tae sometime today. Spin was back in town, but he knew Tae would be good for what he had in mind.

Will wanted to kidnap Hustle's daughter and torture her, just to send Hustle a clear message that he was playing for keeps in the streets.

Pulling into the parking lot, he saw Bank's car. He had to figure out what he was going to do about Agent Moore's wife and him because shit could get deadly if it went wrong. Agent Moore was playing games and trying to set them up.

***

The bangs at the door made Bank jump up from the couch to answer it. He already knew who it was.

"Hold up!" Bank yelled, trying to make Will wait just like he would make him wait.

"God damn! What the fuck you in here doing jerking off?" Will entered, strolling past Bank at the door.

"I was laying down in the living room, but what's going on?"

"You need to clean this bitch up," Will said as he stepped over boxes of pizza, beers, bottles of liquor and wrappers.

"I'ma have that chick do it," Bank said.

"Where is she?"

"Sleeping," Bank replied.

"Her husband got the file, so now we just play it by ear," Will said.

"By ear? We need to get that shit," Bank said. Seeing how his attitude was towards his freedom, he was seeing his true side.

"It could be a set up," Will said, sitting down on a couch watching the sports channel.

"I don't think he's crazy," Bank added.

"I know my husband. He did it. He won't cross you. He's addicted to me." Agent Moore's wife came from out back being nosy. She was still cuffed up, but the chain on the cuffs had enough length where she could move around as she needed.

"Bitch, get your ugly ass in the back!" Will shouted, seeing her get off to the back.

"I'ma make sure it's good before we make our move. I don't trust it. He did this shit too fast, but I gotta go holla at Tae. I'ma call you later. Watch her." Will left the crib, leaving him pissed off.

***

Raleigh, N.C.

In Raleigh North Apartments, Tae and his best friend Justin watched how their young boys made sales to fiends and serviced other local drug dealers.

Seeing their hood eat made them feel good. Nobody ever did this for them or da hood, except years ago an African plug named Zayon flooded the hood with dope and weed. Niggas were eating big time. Niggas got greedy and killed Zayon after robbing him. Word on the streets was the nigga who did it was Big Zone.

"This shit changing up, bruh. We went from selling weed, dropping out of school, and robbing to now selling bricks and supplying the hood," Justin said blowing weed smoke out his mouth watching the apartments.

It was 7 p.m., so the street lights were on, at least the ones that worked and there was a cookout going on in the park across the street. The smell of barbecue could be smelled all through the hood.

"Fact," Tae replied, thinking the same thing about how far they had come.

"What's going on with Low Dee?" Justin knew Low Dee's game was heavy for busting his gun, but he wasn't as close to him as Tae was because they were family.

"I gotta go see him one of these days. I just been so focused on a bag, bro."

"We need to fly out somewhere. We need a vacation," Justin said.

"I'm down for Atlanta or Miami."

Tae said, checking his Rolex watch, waiting on his uncle.

Will called him earlier telling him he needed to get up with him around seven tonight, so Tae told him to come out to the hood so they could link up. Tae hoped it was a big move, so he could put more drugs in the hood and do him.

Now he was buying bricks from Will here and there. He was ok with that, but his wolves were hungry and howling.

"Atlanta, bro," Justin said, getting pumped up thinking about hitting up Magic City, Onyx, and Blue Flame out in da ATL.

"We sliding in a few days, but let me see what this nigga want."

Tae saw his uncle's luxury car pull up across the street.

Tae crossed the street wondering what Will had in mind because Tae's main task was still Big Zone. But Big Zone was smart and playing chess, so Tae had been trying to beat him at his own game with real patience.

"Nephew."

"Uncle."

"Why your young boy be ice grilling?" Will asked, always seeing Justin mean mugging him.

"Ask him," Tae shot back, knowing Will ain't finna jump the gun with some young turnt up savages.

"Nah, it's cool. Just watch him. There is something about him. I see it in his eyes," Will told his nephew.

Tae was thinking in his head how Justin said the same shit about Will to him on a regular basis.

"What's going on? Why you call?"

"I need a favor," Will said.

"I'm listening."

"Hustle put more money on my head."

"How much?" Tae asked, sounding as if he was interested.

"I don't know. Why you ask?"

"Just a question, but I'm sure you ain't call me to tell me this." Tae looked at Will because Will had sneaky ways of saying shit and doing shit so Tae was always on alert.

"Hustle got a daughter and I want you to kidnap her for me, and I'll handle the rest," Will said.

"Iight," Tae replied nonchalantly.

"Easy. That's why I love you, nephew." Will smiled, knowing Tae was down.

"100,000."

"What? You charging after all I did for you!" Will got upset.

"Nigga, I put in my own work. You not out here in the field like me so 100,000 or find somebody else," Tae told him, seeing his uncle's face tighten.

"I'll have the money to you tomorrow, and I will text you the chick's workplace. She drives a white Mercedes AMG sedan. I hear she's a bad bitch. I can't wait to kill her and send her body to him."

"That's between you and dude. I'ma do my part. Just have my paper, OG." Tae left the car laughing.

Will stared at Tae crossing the street and then at Justin thinking Tae was starting to get too big headed and ungrateful. He also felt he was doing something sneaky, but he pulled off coming up with his own personal plan for Tae and Justin.

Chapter 29
Durham, N.C.

Scrilla and Main posted up on Drive Street, located on the Eastside of town. They both had been so busy lately that crossing paths was rare for them.

"What's up with your little sister? I saw her a few days ago in the mall," Scrilla said, watching the block jump with fiends tonight.

Main had a lot of Crip homies on this side of town, so he began opening shop and making big money moves.

"She good in school trying to do the right thing, cuz," Main said, seeing a text from his auntie and niece who needed him to come pick them up from church.

"I ain't heard nothing from this clown M.I. or YN have you?" Scrilla asked because shit had been too quiet for the past few weeks.

"Nah."

"Be on point. Dem boys sneaky," Scrilla stated.

"I know cuz, but I'ma need some more work soon." Main was running low on product

"Iight. Give me a few days, bro."

"That shit moving out here, cuz." Main saw a thick chick walk past pushing a baby stroller with a phat ass.

"I see, nigga. There is a fucking fiend on every corner." Scrilla knew his city was the dope capital of the state.

Scrilla knew that with the right plug he could really make millions in his city because he had his crew.

"I gotta slide across town. You going to that big party in Diamond Girl?" Main asked, knowing everybody was going to be at that club later for the biggest party of the city.

"Diamond Girl?" Scrilla forgot it, about it because he wasn't a party type nigga.

"Yeah, I was thinking about going out there wit a few Loc's," Main said, needing some time out.

"Everybody gonna be there, huh?" Scrilla's mind went into overdrive as he came up with a quick idea.

"Facts. The whole city," Main said before it finally hit him.

"You thinking what I'm thinking?" Scrilla stated, looking at Main.

"Facts, bruh. Let's do it. I know one of them fools gonna be there, cuz," Main said.

"I'ma plot some shit out, but I'ma call you two hours before the party so we can go over the details." Scrilla smiled, feeling brilliant.

"I'll be ready. Just hit me." Main climbed in his car pulling off.

***

West End Durham

Main raced to pick up his auntie and 13 year old niece from church thinking about tonight's event at the club.

He had a strong feeling M.I. and YN would be there live and present because they loved to be the center of attention, unlike his 700 Block shooters.

Since Scrilla got on, shit had been different for Main and his crew. Getting money felt so good, but one thing Main knew about the game is that good things don't last forever, so he had been focused on saving money for a rainy day.

As he pulled into the busy church parking lot, he saw a few bad chicks, but one really caught his eyes. She was walking to her car alone with a baby in her arms and a baby bag in her arm.

Main threw the car in park to help her real quick like a true gentleman.

"Let me help you." Main saw the woman trying to open the back door to her newest modeled Acura sedan.

"Thank you so much," she said, placing her baby in the car seat. She bent over enough just to give him a clear look at her phat ass.

Main couldn't help but to stare at her big ass. She blocked the car door with her wide hips.

"Thanks again." The woman closed the door and looked at him with her chink eyes. She was a bad bitch who got her body done after having a child.

"No problem, beautiful."

"Maybe we can get up one day," she said with no shame, writing down her name and number on a piece of paper.

"I'm wit that." Main couldn't believe how easy it was to bag the sexy woman.

"Cool. Hit me when you ready." The woman climbed in the car leaving.

Main saw his aunt and little niece coming towards him as he placed the piece of paper in his pocket.

"Auntie," Main said, approaching his aunt and niece, but unaware of the truck lurking behind him.

***

YN couldn't believe he saw Main in a church parking lot out of all places as he was on his way to Gunna Street to check on his little homie who owed him a few bands. He was with two shooters in the SUV when he saw the chick with the phatty get in the car racing off. He knew it was the perfect time to pull up on Main.

"Slow down," YN told his driver as he rolled down the passenger window and stuck a long pipe out of the window.

Bloc...

Bloc...

Bloc...

Bloc...

Bloc...

The gun had double action, so YN didn't have to do much except aim.

He hit Main in his leg and the little girl in the head. By the time Main hit the floor to get his weapon out of the truck, he was already halfway out of the lot. Main's wound wasn't that bad, but he saw his auntie holding his niece's dead bloody body crying. Main saw people surrounding them trying to help while calling the police. Main knew he couldn't stay there and wait for the police to come because he had a gun on him, and people saw him shooting. Going to jail today wasn't in his plans at all. He got up and limped to his car trying not to look back as the EMS truck pulled into the church lot.

***

Chapel Hill, N.C.

Spin was thirty minutes outside of Durham waiting on Will to come through as he waited in a shopping plaza next to North Carolina University.

It was time for him to come back to the city and finish off where he left off.

Spin was in his Nissan getting his dick sucked by a big lip plus-size woman that he met a few days ago with some good wetty and a crazy head game.

The chick bopped her head up and down slurping and moaning.

"Suck that dick good, girl."

"I am, daddy. I wanna drink your cum," she said, coming up for air.

"Fuck … hold that thought," Spin said, seeing Will park across from him. Spin fixed himself up and got out walking to Will's car as he got out of the Maybach.

"What's going on?" Will said.

"Same shit. Living day to day. Good to see you," Spin said, feeling Will's vibe was off a little.

"You clear to come. I took care of that shooting so you're clear. I'ma need you soon. I want you to handle my nephew," Will said.

"What? You mean kill him?"

"Yes."

"Which one?"

"Tae," Will said smoothly, showing his cold side.

"Ok, give me a little time."

"Let him enjoy the summer, so he can continue cleaning up my little mess. Then I want you to do him in good," Will said with a strong tone.

"I got'cha, boss man."

"I know you do, but this is for you to hold you over, but I still want you to lay low for a while." Will handed Spin three wads of money.

"I know. I am. Just hit me when you ready." Spin got out of the car.

"I will youngin," Will stated with a smirk, knowing his plan was coming together.

Romell Tukes

Chapter 30
Downtown Raleigh

Tae slowed the Hellcat wide body down and eased behind traffic on his way to the address his uncle gave him. Looking at the piece of paper, the address looked familiar to him, but he paid it no mind as he thought about his next re-up.

Tae really wasn't feeling Will's energy. He knew soon that he would need to find a new plug. He wanted to stay consistent, so he could feed his team. Killing women was never in his plans. He was totally against it until he started to understand how a nigga would kill or harm his loved ones. He had to get theirs before his enemy came for his.

It was a little after rush hour, so he hoped the woman he came for didn't leave work just yet. Tae already came up with the plan to stalk her to see where she lived, then make his move. The way Will wanted him to do it was dumb and risky. It could've easily landed him in jail if he killed her in broad daylight downtown.

The only thing Will gave him was a work address and a license plate number to figure out whom the woman was he needed Tae to kill. Tae made a left into the parking lot, and he couldn't believe where he was. He had to do a double take on the paper, then up to the building number.

The place of business was a lawyer's office, but not just any lawyer's office but the one his girlfriend Rena worked at. Tae looked at the license plate number on the paper, and then he looked at Rena's Mercedes-Benz's license plate.

"What the fuck?" Tae parked and was shocked to see Rena's license plate number. It was the exact same number that was on the paper.

Tae couldn't believe his uncle tried to get him to kill his girlfriend. All types of crazy thoughts ran through his head. He started thinking Rena was a plug living two different lives. Or she could have been his opp the whole time.

Rena came out of work texting on her phone with her head down smiling at her text. Tae's car was parked in the cut between two cars, so most likely she couldn't be able to see him. When she got in the Benz, he got a text saying: I miss you. I'm about to call. After that text, he got a call. He watched her closely.

"Hey …" He heard her loud ratchet voice.

"What's up, sexy? What you doing?" he questioned.

"Thinking about you."

"Facts. Where you at?"

"I just got off work and Lord knows I'm fucking tired. How about you?" she shot back, parked in the car relaxing after a long day of helping out her racist boss.

"I'm just chilling," he added.

"Chilling uhmmm … I hope you not around no bitches. Matter of fact, put me on speaker," she demanded.

"Iight." He did as she asked.

"Say you miss me and love eating my ass," Rena said.

"Girl, you crazy."

"Say it. I'm not playing, Tae."

"Ok, I miss you and I love eating your ass, baby. I like sucking your toes and the cum out your pussy," Tae said.

"Ewwww … you nasty nasty, babe. That's why I'm falling in love with you." She never said the four letter word until now.

"You falling in love?" He had to make sure he wasn't hearing shit.

"Yeah, I am, but don't get all hype," she said.

"I feel the same, Rena."

"You do?" she asked.

"Yeah, I do."

"You better, but I have to go to my mom's house real quick. I'ma see you tonight."

"Facts."

"I love you, too," he said, seeing her Benz pull out of the parking spot.

Tae hung up and watched her drive off, thinking about how he wasn't going to kill his girl for Will. He wasn't going to let anybody touch her.

Coke Boys

***

Durham, N.C.

Club Diamond Girl was packed tonight and M.I. and his crew were turned up.

Everybody was out and about enjoying the energy of the club. M.I. had his own section with a gang of niggas from his team and YN was standing on a couch turning liquor bottles of Moet upside down dancing and doing his two step.

"Your boy turned up," Tick told M.I. who was to the left of him.

"He deserves it. We all do, bruh. This our city. We run this shit!" M.I. shouted over the loud music.

"This shit for City!" YN shouted as he popped open a bottle of Spade and sprayed it on people. Then, the craziest shit happened in the club.

***

Scrilla, Main, and his 700 Block crew ran through the crowd with night vision goggles and assault rifles on their way to M.I.'s VIP section.

Tatt... Tatt... Tat... Tat... Tatt... Tatt... Tatt...

The gunfire lit the club back up as the crew sprayed into M.I.'s VIP section hitting whoever was in sight.

Tat... Tat... Tat... Tat... Tat... Tat... Tat... Tat...

People yelled, ran, screamed, and cried, trying to get away from the mass shooting. M.I. and YN crawled out of the section as Tick's body fell in front of them. They left the guns in the car, something they regretted.

The security team at the door was from 700 Block and Scrilla paid them. When they ran up in the club, they shut off the power after seeing where M.I. was located.

By the time the lights came back on, Scrilla and his crew were out of the back door hopping in their cars, racing off four cars deep.

Ten people were wounded, and five people were pronounced dead on the scene. M.I. was one of the people that got shot but YN lucked up. M.I. got hit in his buttocks. The bullet took a piece of flesh off his ass cheek, but the bullet didn't go in.

Chapter 31
Winston, N.C.

"Is this everything, Abdul? Let me know because if I count this shit and ya missing a bill, I'm coming back," Hustle said in his boy Abdul's mansion.

"Nigga, you still owe me five keys from the last shipment, brother," Abdul said, sitting in his kitchen drinking a bottle early in the morning looking over the 120 keys on the table he got from Hustle today.

Abdul had been copping work from Hustle since he got in the game. The two men knew each other for over a decade, and they had a close brotherly relationship. Abdul had a few cities under his wing getting to a bag with his little crew.

"I'll get you on the back end, you rich now. You can't stress the little shit," Hustle replied, being his funny self.

"I bet."

"How the wife and kids?" Hustle asked.

"Everybody good. My wife and kid went out to visit their family in Texas."

"Iight. That's what's up."

"How's your daughter? I ain't see her in years?" Abdul asked.

"She's a lawyer now, well, a paralegal but she doing good. I'm proud of her, man. Real shit, that girl finna be the death of me one day," Hustle said with pride.

"That's great. She learned from the best, but I know you're ready for some grandbabies soon." Abdul finished the bottle.

"Hell, nah."

"You not getting no younger, Hustle."

"I know, but I can't have no grandkids. I'm still in these streets. Ain't no retirement 401K plan out here for us, man. So, before I have grandkids, I want to be able to live in peace. Not in fear," Hustle said.

"I hear that."

"Rena told me she got a boyfriend now, and it's serious." Hustle shook his head, thinking back to when Rena told him she was in a real relationship with a boy from Raleigh.

"Did you check him yet?"

"Not yet, but I plan to soon. I just been doing a lot of shit out of town trying to get shit right."

"You need to stay on that because nowadays, the young boys are built different," Abdul said.

"I agree."

"You still be fucking around in Durham?" Abdul asked.

"Yeah, that's my stomping ground," Hustle boasted.

"You saw what happened on the news the other day?"

"No."

"There was a mass shooting in one of them clubs. The news said a gang of shooters ran up in the club like professional hit squad niggas shutting off the lights and airing shit out killing a rack of muthafuckers," Abdul stated.

"Damn. Durham turned up."

"Bull City always been wild since we was kids." Abdul called Durham by its nickname Bull City.

"I gotta go." Hustle looked at his bust down watch, then closed the briefcase filled with the money he got from Abdul.

"Come back soon," Abdul said.

"I got you, old man."

"It's gonna be Chess' birthday in a few days. Will you be good?" Abdul asked, knowing how sad Hustle got around Chess' birthday. Abdul used to sell for Chess. He showed Abdul the game.

"I'll be good." Hustle left thinking about the man who killed his brother, Will.

Hustle had been waiting on the right time to get at Will, but he had been hearing a lot of talk about him in the streets. Dealing with a man like Will, a person had to have patience and outsmart him because Will was a smart snake.

***

Coke Boys

Duke Hospital, Durham

M.I. left the hospital with a cane because after being shot it fucked up his walk. His little nephew was fighting for his life since the club shooting for a few days.

A few minutes ago, his nephew died in his sleep and M.I. was crushed because he felt like it was his fault even bringing a sixteen-year-old out to the club, but he was trying to be a good uncle. M.I. already figured that his opp Scrilla did that bullshit. Now he was rolling around a few cars deep with security, just in case he saw any of Scrilla's people. M.I. was really scared of the young wild niggas after the club shooting because they were young and ruthless. YN was parked in the front of the hospital with a truck parked behind him and two cars behind that.

"What happened?" YN asked when M.I. got inside of the SUV.

"He ain't make it."

"Damn."

"Find this little nigga's family and make them suffer," M.I. stated in a cold tone.

"Got you." YN pulled off.

***

Rocky Mountain, N.C.

Agent Moore had been geeking to get his wife back in one piece tonight. He drove out to a Home Depot parking lot in Rocky Mountain to meet with Will and Bank. He had been waiting for a few days now to hand over the material he stole from his boss' office. Two days ago, his boss almost flipped the office looking for the files because Will's caseload was erased from his computer. That made him pissed off. Moore tried to help his boss find Will and Bank's file, but they came up empty handed. Agent Moore took a few days off from work because he had a lot going on, dealing with his wife and the criminals. He had to sit and wait until Will called him, so he could get his wife back. When Will called that morning and told him to meet him in a parking lot at night he was eager. Moore was ten minutes early hoping everything went well. After this incident, he thought about quitting the FBI because he didn't want to put his life at risk again.

***

Bank drove the van with Will in the passenger seat, silently listening to Moore's wife in the backseat asking the same question over twenty times.

"Where are we going? Please kill *him*, not me. I know nothing about this," Moore's wife cried.

"Shut up. Damn!" Will shouted, turning around.

"Sorry," she cried.

The van pulled into the Home Depot parking lot to see it was half empty besides the overnight employee's cars.

"Iight." Bank parked next to the navy-blue Impala with dark tint.

Agent Moore got out of the car with a folder in his hand and had a scared look on his face.

"Let's make this fast," Will said, getting out and letting his wife out of the side door, but she was cuffed up like a prisoner.

"You got the shit?" Bank asked.

"I'll do the talking. You got the shit?" Will said.

"Yes, here it is, and I erased all the files on my boss' computer," Agent Moore said.

"How do we know you deleted it?" Will asked.

"This is a text from him asking me what happened to the files." Moore showed them both the text from his boss.

"Ok, that's fair. I believe you. Good job," Will said, handing him back his phone.

"Come on, baby!" Agent Moore said seeing Bank uncuff her. When he saw his wife standing there smiling brightly, something awkward came over him.

"I don't think so," Moore's wife said, taking Bank's pistol and aiming it at her husband, seeing the confused look on his face.

"What's going on?" Agent Moore looked sick.

"This was a setup, dummy. I've been fucking Will for 10 years. I'm the one who told him you were on to them. This was my idea and damn you're slow. I hate you," she said, seeing tears fall from his eyes.

"Bitch," Moore stated.

Boc. Boc. Boc. Boc. Boc. Boc. Boc. Boc. Boc.

Moore's wife fired bullets in his face, killing her husband with a smile. She had been dreaming of this day for years.

Romell Tukes

Chapter 32
Raleigh, N.C.

Will was in the backseat of the car, getting the best head he ever had in his life. Now, Will understood why the late Agent Moore was in love with his wife. Her head bobbed up and down in his lap, making loud slurp sounds.

"Damn, bitch," Will moaned.

"You like?" She stopped, lifting her head up.

"Finish up." He forced her head back down onto his cock.

When he shot his load into her mouth, she swallowed it all with one gulp.

"I'm so happy he's out of the picture. Now we can live our lives happily." She was fucking all his friends, family members, and co-workers. When she had the chance to get away from him with Will, she took the chance and had no problem with pulling the trigger to show her love.

"Me, too."

"Now you can fuck me all day," Kim whispered in his ear.

"I know."

"I want to fuck you right now," she said as she tried to climb on his lap.

"Oh, hold on."

"What's wrong?" she asked, unaware that the car made a right on to a dark country road leading into a lake.

"I got a surprise for you, Kim." Will smiled looking at her big breasts he liked.

"Where are we going?" She got nervous looking out of the car window.

"It's a surprise." He then talked to Bank. "Bank, right here is good," Will said, able to see a small lake on the trail's path.

"Iightt." Bank knew Will like the back of his hand, so he played on his phone.

"Come on, baby," Will said.

"I always wanted to do this," she said, jumping out of the car.

Kim and Will walked towards the lake, and she wasted no time getting naked, then getting on her knees. When she latched on to suck his dick, he pulled out a gun.

BOOM!!

BOOM!!

Will shot her in the forehead twice and saw her body slowly drop to the floor before he walked off.

"That bitch got the best head I ever had in my life," Will said, shaking his head.

"Why you ain't keep her?" Bank backed out into the highway.

"She would've snitched."

"You think?"

"Hell yeah, Bank."

"Why you say that? She seemed pretty solid," Bank added.

"Let me tell you something my old head used to tell me. Never trust a married bitch who is disloyal to her husband because she will be disloyal to you," Will said the same thing Chess used to tell him about women back in the day.

"That makes sense," Bank said.

"It sure does, youngin. It sure does," Will said twice, staring out of the window of the car thinking about his future take over in N.C.

***

Durham, N.C.

Since the club shooting M.I. had been laying low because the FEDS, DEA, ATF, and local police had their nose into his shit, so he had to close shop for a few weeks. M.I. was still pissed off about being shot in the ass that night in the club, but a lot of his goons lost their lives, so he was very grateful to be alive.

He knew Scrilla and his boyz did it because the shooting was too perfect. M.I. had to give it to the young niggas the way they set that whole shit up was on point.

The club shooting was still the talk of the town and M.I. knew he had to do something quick, but first he needed a plan and a good one.

Today he had to meet his plug at a small restaurant he always drove by, and he had to come alone in his Cadillac. M.I. missed his little brother Moez. He only had YN left and he tried to stay on his toes because they could not afford to take any L's.

M.I. parked in front of the restaurant and walked inside to see only a few customers. His plug was sitting at a table next to the wall eating eggs and sausages.

"What's up, bossman?" M.I. asked Hustle, whose face was serious.

"Sit the fuck down," Hustle said as M.I. did what he was told.

"Everything, ok?" M.I. didn't know why Hustle asked him to come out today. He rarely talked or called M.I. unless it was time for a shipment.

"No, it's not, fool."

"I did something? I sent you all the money I owed."

"It's not the fucking money," Hustle shot back.

"What's the problem?"

"Let me ask you a question, how smart are you really?"

"Huh?"

"Answer my damn question. I'ma get to my damn point," Hustle stated, very upset.

"I'm very smart. I been in this game long enough to know how to move." M.I. didn't have a clue where this was going, but he knew it wasn't good.

"Ok, good answer. If you're so fucking smart how did you get shot in your ass in a club? If you're so smart, why is the fucking feds on my tail breathing down my neck? If you're so fucking smart how was the feds able to hit my last shipment two days ago? I'ma tell you where you come in this situation at M.I. I have people on the payroll, and they told me two things." Hustle paused as he leaned back.

M.I. sat there with a dumbfounded look on his face. This was all new to him, but he knew his plug had the right to be upset.

"First, they said you been drawing heat to my organization. Next, you have a family member snitching to the feds and a nigga in your camp snitching to the DEA," Hustle said.

"A family member?"

"Yes, the man's name is Ronny."

"My stepdad?" M.I. couldn't believe it was his stepdad who raised him and YN. He used to be a pimp too.

"The person in your crew is named Dusty." Hustle remembered at the top of his head.

"Fuck." M.I. knew Dusty. He was YN's best friend for over a decade.

"Handle this and fall back for a while." Hustle got up to leave, storming out of the place.

Chapter 33
Southside, Durham

Scrilla called a big meeting in one of his boys' mom's backyard next to Fargo Projects that his 700 Block crew had on lock.

There were over forty people in the backyard wondering what the fuck was going on, looking at Scrilla and Main post up in front of everybody.

Main had been taking a lot of family losses lately and it had been affecting him big time to the point all he could think or talk about was killing niggas from the other side.

Scrilla somewhat felt his best friend's pain. Main was the one who hit M.I. in the ass, but both men were a little upset that YN or M.I. didn't get murked instead a bunch of nobody's.

Everybody down with 700 Block was mostly gangbanging GDs and Crips with a few Bloods but very few. Scrilla loved his crew because everybody was down to kill and drill. Now niggas had been getting money. They had been taking over certain areas in the city.

"Listen up, ya'll!" Main shouted because it was loud, and it was time to start their meeting.

"Everybody out'cha looking like money 700 Block shit, this is all we got. We family. Let's value that shit. Anyway, I called niggas out to inform ya'll we about to step our game up. Anytime you see an opportunity in life, you have to take it head on," Scrilla said.

Main didn't even know what Scrilla was talking about. He looked confused, just like the rest of the crew.

"As we all know about the ongoing beefing with M.I. and YN, we about to hit dem boyz hard. You feel me? They been closing down shop lately, and we about to open up shop on their blocks," Scrilla said smiling.

"How?" someone in the crowd asked out loud.

"I'ma send five soldiers to each of their hoods and projects. We gonna spin their blocks, look for any opps outside and if you see any, lay them down then the next morning open shop bright and early. If nobody out, post up and let niggas know we looking for new recruits and we taking over. Get wit us or go against us," Scrilla said, seeing a lot of his crew nod their heads.

"That's the end of the meeting. Y'all know how we coming," Main said as the crew split up. Some left, others chilled, plotted, and smoked weed.

***

Eastside, Durham

"This finna be fast, bruh," YN told his boy Dusty as they got out of a GMC Sedan parked on the corner in front of a two-story house.

"What's the plot, homie?" Dusty asked, tucking his gun in his lower back side.

"I don't know," YN said, wondering why Dusty was asking so many questions, something he never used to do.

"Who crib is this?" Dusty asked.

"Nigga, just follow my lead." YN walked up the stairs.

YN had been peeping a lot of funny shit with Dusty lately. Dusty had been playing hide and seek for the past couple of weeks and acting different.

They were childhood friends, so they knew each other better than anybody did.

"Iight." Dusty looked around nervously, hoping this wasn't a set-up he was walking into.

Four months ago, Dusty got pulled over coming out of his projects with a Draco assault rifle and two keys of dope and two keys of coke in his car.

When he got booked, the DEA also raided his crib to find four and a half bricks of coke and more guns with lasers and night vision scopes. Dusty also had extended clips on everything.

With his back against the wall, Dusty couldn't stand the pressure when they started to talk football numbers.

YN knocked on the front door, and he heard gospel music playing from inside the house.

"Play it cool," YN told Dusty, seeing him sweat bullets.

"I'm good, bro," Dusty lied, praying YN didn't do a crime in front of him because he would have to snitch on his childhood friend. Dusty already told on M.I. and Main, but he didn't want to tell on YN, but he also didn't want to be pressured.

An old woman in a cooking apron opened the door.

"I'm cooking now, grand babe." The older woman thought it was her grandchild Scrilla coming over like he asked. When she saw it wasn't Scrilla she raised her eyebrows.

"Go inside," YN said.

"Excuse me," she said before seeing YN's gun slap her across her face.

The elder woman's body flew to the floor as they rushed the crib and closed the door behind them.

"Where is Scrilla?" YN shouted, turning into a monster with red eyes.

"Please, I'm a God fearing woman!" she cried out from the floor.

Dusty just stood there, not knowing what to do, and his boy saw this.

"I'm bout to ask you one more time. Where is he?" YN cocked his gun back.

"Tell him Miss," Dusty said as YN looked at him oddly.

"Nigga, what the fuck you on, bruh?" YN asked.

"Helping," Dusty shot back.

"I don't know, and if I did, I would never give my grandbabies up," she said.

"Oh, is that right?" YN replied with an evil smirk.

Boc...

Boc...

Boc...

Boc...

The bullet hit the woman in the lower stomach, hitting a few organs, killing her slowly.

YN and Dusty walked out of the crib, but something was bothering YN and he couldn't let it go.

"Why you acting funny?"

"Huh?" Dusty replied.

"Bruh, you buggin. You on some weird shit," YN said.

"I'm cool."

"You sure?"

"Yeah, I'm just tired, bro. I'ma go home and get some sleep," Dusty lied. What was really on his mind was if he should report what he just saw.

"I'll drop you off." YN felt the strange vibe but blocked the thoughts.

Chapter 34
Eastside, Durham

Scrilla and Main were on his way to his grandmom's crib for dinner. When he pulled down her block, he went by a familiar car speeding by him, but he paid the car no mind.

"Why she not answering?" Scrilla asked, calling his grandmom's phone.

His sister was supposed to come up from Atlanta to spend the week with him and the family, but he hadn't heard from her either, which was weird.

"She may be cooking. You know how she do, bru," Main stated, loving his grandmom's cooking.

Main used to always come over to Scrilla's grandmom's crib after church on Sunday's to eat when his late grandmom wasn't cooking up a storm.

"Yeah, she may be blasting that gospel shit." Scrilla laughed, parked outside of the two-story home his grandmom had been living in since he was a little nigga.

"Facts," Main said, thinking about his mom who he missed.

Scrilla walked up the stairs and realized the front door was wide open.

When he walked deeper into the crib, he saw his grandmom lying dead in a puddle of blood.

Tears rolled down Scrilla's face. That was his only reaction because he knew the only reason she got killed was because of his drama.

Growing up, she used to always tell him he would be the death of her one day, and that became true.

"What the fuck?" Main walked inside the house to see the body.

Main couldn't believe what he saw. Never in a million years would Main have imagined Scrilla's church going grandmom would've been murdered cold blooded.

Scrilla turned and walked out with no words. He just wiped his tears and held his head high.

Main felt for his boy. He read his expression and saw how hurt he really was, but he knew it had just released the beast that was deep within.

***

North Carolina State University, Chapel Hill

"Bri, I get paid in two days. I swear, I'll pay you," a young white male student said in his dorm room.

"I don't know, Chad," Bri said.

"Bri, I always pay."

"Yes, but you know I do straight business, no cut," she stated, checking her watch.

Bri's brother was waiting for her in the parking lot, so she could re-up and talk with him.

"I'm charging you double then, Chad," she told him.

"Ok, I'ma need it for the party," Chad told her.

Bri pulled out two ounces of coke and a hundred pills from her purse and placed it on the table.

"Have my money, Chad."

"I will, Bri."

"I know you will. Have fun." Bri walked out before the young man took a quick peep at her sexy body, wishing he could taste her, but she didn't fuck with anybody on campus for some reason.

Bri rushed to the parking lot in her heels with her purse filled with stacks of money.

Since Bri had been at school, she had been getting to a bag. Bri was making at least 8 -10,000 dollars a day on campus, and she loved it.

Thanks to Tae, she was doing big things. She was seeing so much money, she would get scared. She had over 100,000 in her purse for Tae to re-up, and she had plans to go car shopping with her profit that she had been saving.

Bri had recently met a nigga, and they were vibing, but she was too busy on a bag and trying to get her money up.

150

Her grades were A's and B's and that kept the school officials off her radar. She was moving smart and like a boss.

***

Tae pulled up behind his goons, who were carrying the drugs in the truck.

When his sister called requesting more product, he was more than happy to bring her some, and he tossed her some extra work because he liked what she was doing.

Seeing her get to a bag made him want to help as much as he could, but he just wanted her to be smart and hustle under the radar.

He saw Bri entering the lot in heels and a dress as if she was going out to a club.

"What's up, ugly?" Bri said, getting into the car of her brother's Hellcat and liking the smell of it.

"Where you going? To a club my nigga? Our lace front fucked up." Tae and his sister always joked since they were kids.

"Ha … Ha … Ha … not funny, but what's going on back home?" she asked.

"Same shit, sis, trying to run it up and stay alive at the same time. You feel me?" Tae said, not trying to worry his sister with his real issues in the streets.

"Stay safe, but I'm trappin hard. I got this shit booming out here bro, facts. I can make a million in a month in this bitch. I never knew so many college kids did hardcore drugs."

"Me either." Tae never knew little smart college kids were fiends.

"I literally saw one kid sniff a whole ounce in less than two minutes," Bri said.

"Damn, but how much you got for me today?" Tae rubbed his hands.

"100,000," she said, going in her purse pulling out stacks of money wrapped in rubber bandz.

"Damn, you racked up."

"Boss bitch shit. Money goals," she replied, handing him the money.

"In the truck in front of me, my goons got a backpack full of keys and pills and I hooked you up," Tae said, thinking about his next re-up because he was dry now.

"Thank you. Nice doing business with you. Love you," she said, opening the door.

"You be careful for real, Bri."

"I will, boy. Bye." Bri knew how to mack, and she didn't need him to tell her.

Raleigh, N.C.

Big Zone was at his sister Winny's crib chilling with her, something he hadn't done in a long time.

Big Zone had been losing family and friends since the beef with the young niggas, so he had to value the little family he did have, and that was his sister Winny.

"Why you single?" Big Zone saw how beautiful his sister was and miserable at the time.

"I don't need a nigga," she shot back pouring herself a drink.

"Iight."

"Really, I'm in a good space."

"That's what your mouth say."

"Niggas got too much baggage, look at you," she said.

"What about me?" Big Zone took that as offensive, plus, he had been drinking all day.

"You in the streets, crazy, stressful, a vicious liar and cheater. Who needs that shit?"

"Point made." He laughed.

"When you gonna leave that street life alone?" she asked.

"I may not ever." He got serious.

"Bro, you up. What more can you ask for? Anything else would be greed," Winny said, sitting down.

"I gotta finish what I started, but I gotta go." Big Zone got up to leave.

Outside, Big Zone's soldiers awaited him, unaware he was being followed all day.

Romell Tukes

Chapter 35
East, Durham

High Park had three of YN's workers outside slanging dope. The area was filled with fiends and gangbangers all day long.

The block was kinda dead tonight, so everybody had plans to go over to Driver Street for a house party.

The past two weeks, YN and M.I.'s blocks had been being taken over by The 700 Block niggas, and they were bodying shit all over town.

M.I. just opened back up shop last week and all his men were being killed left and right. He didn't know what was going on, but he knew who was causing all the mayhem.

M.I. only had three hoods left around the city that were still his and wasn't D-bo'd by his opps.

"I think I got a sell pulling up. After this, we can go," PC said, seeing a car slowly pull up to the block.

When the Chevy Malibu came to a halt, four doors slowly opened, and then shit got real in a matter of seconds.

Tat...

Tat...

Tat...

Tat...

Tat...

Tat...

Tat...

Tat...

Tat...

Main and his goon aired the block out, hitting all four men, killing them. Main saw one of the men was his little sister's boyfriend, but it was too late.

They hopped back in the car, driving off.

"Tomorrow, y'all take over this hood," Main told them as they drove back to their block.

"We on it, bru," the driver said, ready to get to a bag.

Scrilla was at his grandmom's funeral today, so he was taking care of business for his boy. They already took over half of the city because M.I. had a lot of areas on lock, which were now run by 700 Block.

***

Northside, Durham

Scrilla stood at his grandmom's casket deep in the ground on this rainy day and couldn't help but feel like the weight of the world was on his shoulder.

Losing his grandmom was rough because she basically helped raise him and his sister because his mom was a fiend his whole life, so his g-mom stepped up and played her role.

Scrilla had been standing there for 20 minutes after the funeral service in the graveyard doing a lot of thinking about the future.

He was now doing shit on another level, and he had to level up because he knew there were people depending on him nowadays.

Taking over M.I.'s blocks was a smart idea, but he knew that for every action, there was a reaction.

"Scrilla, how you feel?" Olivia asked, walking up behind her brother dressed in all black with a black sun hat with an umbrella in her hand. It wasn't raining hard, only lightly today.

"I haven't seen you in a while," Scrilla said, not even looking at her.

"I know. I've been a little busy, but my number is still the same," Olivia said because her brother never called.

"Fo 'sho."

"I can't believe someone killed granny. I remember that time we was baking cookies, and you almost burned the house down. She came downstairs and asked, who smoking that weed shit?" Olivia remembered making Scrilla smile because he never forgot that funny day. "She was crazy but fair. She had a good heart."

"Facts, but how come you ain't come out for the service part? They had some good stories. It almost made me cry," Scrilla told her because everybody knew he wasn't the type to cry.

"Not tough Scrilla."

"Yeah, my eyes got a little wet," he shot back.

"I don't like funerals, but grandmom was my everything," Olivia said, looking at the ground where her grandmom was lowered.

"I know what you mean," Scrilla replied because funerals always gave him goosebumps.

"How's life out here? It looks like you doing good for yourself." Olivia looked at his Dolce and Gabbana outfit and Cuban link chain.

"I'm doing good, but how's school? When you graduating?"

"I been meaning to tell you that I been slowing down on school and shit," she said.

"Why?"

"I been working overnights," she said, hoping he would leave it at that.

"Doing what?" he asked, sounding happy that Olivia was working and focused on school.

"At a club."

"A club? What, you're a bartender?"

"Not really."

"What you be doing?" Scrilla didn't even wanna think of the worst, not just yet.

"I'm a dancer."

"Like a stripper?"

"Yes, Scrilla. You know what a dancer is." Olivia would never lie to her brother.

"Why? You don't have to do that." Scrilla was furious, but he controlled it.

"Yes I do. Its good money."

"Find a regular job."

"Fuck, no. I like my job, Scrilla. I conduct myself like a real woman should. Scrilla, I know what I'm doing." She was starting

157

to get upset because she was grown and didn't need his input on shit.

"I'll send you money."

"I don't want your money."

"It's not about that, Olivia."

"I have to go. I'ma call you when I get back to Atlanta." Olivia walked off as it started to rain a little harder and her heels started to sink down in the mud.

Scrilla watched his sister struggle to walk away, and he had to get out of the rain. Scrilla had too much shit to focus on besides Olivia, so he left the funeral and focused on new goals.

Coke Boys

Chapter 36
Atlanta, GA

Will arrived in Atlanta a few hours ago to visit his plug, who was his blood brother, one of many he had scattered around the south. Getting out of North Carolina was the right time because a lot was going on and things weren't going as he planned with M.I. and Big Zone.

He knew Hustle was on his line and wanted him dead and would do anything to make that shit happen, so he wasn't lacking. Bank and Spin were running the show while he was gone.

Bank was one of the most trusted men he knew, and Spin was like family to him. He loved the little nigga. He basically showed him the game.

Supplying Scrilla and Tae was becoming a handful because they were starting to get to a real bag. He found himself re-up daily now, at least once a week he had to put in an order.

Will drove a rental to a condo in the downtown area where Buzz lived with his brother.

After the meeting, he planned to hit up a few clubs and get litty by himself for his birthday weekend.

Will's birthday was today, but he was to the point in life where birthdays were just a regular day.

The condo building was large and fancy. Will laughed because every time he came to Atlanta, his brother had a new spot.

In the building, Will took the elevator to the penthouse suite, as his brother requested. Will was getting big money, but he knew to live in some shit like this he would go broke eventually.

Living a luxurious lifestyle was something he used to dream about growing up, especially seeing niggas like Chess slide through in big Cadillacs, and Lincolns back in the days.

At times, he would think about how he snaked his role model, but he remembered one day Chess told him if a man got snaked then he deserved it. When Will asked who, Chess told him every animal must adapt to his habitat.

Will got off on the penthouse floor, laughing to himself, seeing a doorman posted up as if the president were inside.

"Buzz inside?" Will asked as the man got on his walkie-talkie with a serious pose.

Seconds later, the door opened and Buzz stood there with a big smile.

"Welcome to my crib," Buzz said, opening his arms as if he was on MTV Cribs.

"Negro, please. Let me in this bitch," Will stated, walking inside on the marble floor, looking at the windows and glass ceiling above his head.

"How you like it?" Buzz asked, wearing a Versace robe.

"Nice."

"Nigga, this spot 9.7 million. Fuck nice. This shit is off the meat rack, but come into my den," Buzz said, leading the way.

Buzz was one of the biggest plugs in Atlanta. He had his niece Ashanti making him a lot of paper.

"You living large." Will knew Buzz loved his ego stroked since a kid.

"I'm trying."

"I see, but let's get to it. I have shit to do."

"Don't rush business," Buzz said, taking a seat in his 10,000 chair.

"How the family down here?" Will asked because he had not visited this side of his fam in a while.

"Everybody good, but Jason got booked for some murders, but besides that I have no clue. I stay in my money lane. Will, you know what I'm about, shawty."

"I dig it."

"How the fam in Raleigh and Durham?" Buzz asked.

"Everybody straight, feel me?"

"Good. I'ma have your order ready for you tonight. You gonna drive back to N.C. wit it?" Buzz laughed.

"Hell, nah."

"Joking."

"I know you are, fool."

"I'ma have my people hit the road tonight with it. I got you, shawty." Buzz always kept his word.

"Thanks, but I'ma go enjoy it alone," Will stated.

"I'ma take you out. I'ma shut down Magic City and Blue Flame for you tonight, and I'm not taking no for an answer."

"Iight man, but I'm rolling dolo. You not finna get one shoot up this time," Will said, referring to the last time he came down to Atlanta. A nigga shot at them in a club, almost killing them both.

"You good. You with the king of the city, and I'm bringing out fifty shooters," Buzz said, pouring himself a drink.

"Iight, only tonight."

"Gotcha birthday boy, and you still ugly as hell," Buzz joked with his sense of humor.

"Fuck you," Will shot back, ready to party.

***

Durham, N.C.

YN climbed in his GMC truck leaving his boy Cee J's house who just came home from the feds after doing six years. Cee J was under house arrest, so YN and M.I. had to go see him because he couldn't leave the crib.

YN never understood niggas who came fresh home and wanted to get back in the field. Cee J was one of them niggas, so YN gave him two pistols and a half of brick of dog food, so he could get right.

Today was Dusty's baby shower, and he wondered why he didn't call him. It was strange, so he was going over there with a 5,000 gift for his babygirl.

Having to find out about his baby shower from social media, and that fucked him up.

Driving to the west end section of town, he stopped at an Exxon gas station to get some gas real quick.

In his tank was a quarter tank, something he never did, but he let one of his bitches use the truck, so he wasn't ever mad because shawty's pussy was grade A.

YN saw a familiar white Impala on 28 inch rims parked in the cut and as he got a closer look at it, he realized it was Dusty's car.

YN was glad his boy was there, so he could see what was really going on with him and the weird vibes.

Parking at pump number four, he saw Dusty in a blue undercover cop car talking to a white man in a suit.

"Oh, shit." YN couldn't believe what he was seeing now. Everything started to add up and piece together.

A few days ago, YN got a new phone, so he hadn't spoken to M.I. but word was he had been looking for him.

YN saw Dusty and the white man going back and forth, then he saw Dusty take a wire connected to a small mic, and YN already knew what that meant his ex-friend was about to cross him.

Not knowing what to do, he slowly backed out and made his way back across town on his way to M.I.'s crib to get his brother's insight on what he just saw.

Chapter 37
North Raleigh, N.C.

Justin had bagged a nice redbone chick he met a few days ago at a rap concert. He knew the chick forever, and he always wanted to fuck, but she used to laugh at him.

When she saw Justin dripping in jewelry and Dior, she hopped on his dick with no shame, especially when she saw his creamy-white big body BMW.

Justin had a new apartment and had been stacking big paper. The money he was getting had been from the work his crew had been selling throughout the city. His plan was to lock down the city, but there were a few roadblocks.

Big Zone and Lil Flex had been a pain in his ass lately, mainly Lil Flex who was Big Zone's worker and shooter from a hood called NBA on the Southside.

A few nights ago, one of Justin's young soldiers got caught slipping outside of a club and was shot sixteen times by the NBA niggas.

Justin told Tae what happened. Tae told him it was on sight for any of them niggas, and that was music to Justin's ears.

He slowed the car down in a section called Lil Mexico in the southeast area, which was the address the chick gave him.

Justin felt there was something wrong because not too many blacks lived around the area where the redbone chick told him to meet her.

"What the fuck?" Justin said to himself, turning down the music and parking in front of a project building to see nobody outside at the moment, which was odd to him.

All of a sudden, a black car with bright hood lights crept up the block but Justin was so busy texting the chick, he didn't see it.

Before Justin could even lift his head up, it was too late.

Lil Flex and another man hung out of the window with AK-47 assault rifles.

Tat...

Tat...

Tat…

Tat…

Tat…

Tat…

Tat…

Tat…

Two bullets hit Justin in his side before the car drove off, and Lil Flex shouted "NBA" out of the window.

Justin was in pain, but he was able to pull off. He knew a hospital was a few blocks away, so he tried his best to remain awake, but he felt himself getting very dizzy.

In a matter of two minutes, Justin made it to the hospital, parked at the exit, and rushed inside holding his side to stop the heavy blood flow.

As soon as Justin stepped foot in there, he passed out. The nurses and regular civilians in the waiting room rushed to Justin's aid.

A pretty brown-skinned chick knew him from her hood. She was there with her son, who cut his hand. She saw Justin's gun about to fall out of his lower back, so she took it from him so he wouldn't get in trouble.

After the hospital workers brought Justin to the back, the brown-skinned chick called Justin's little sister, who she was cool with to tell her about what happened.

One thing she knew was if Tae found out about this, he would spazz out and turn the city upside down. She saw a nigga try to play Tae one day, and he killed him in front of everybody, so she knew whoever did that to Justin was in for it.

***

North Raleigh, N.C.

Tae had just hung up the phone with Justin's sister, who told him Justin got shot up and was rushed to surgery to remove the bullets.

"Justin got hit up, bruh. We gotta go," Tae told the six troops sitting in the apartment building, chilling.

Niggas grabbed their weapons, and all ran for the door, ready to clean some shit up.

On Tae's way to the hospital, all he could think about was who did this to his boy. He was ready to blow some shit up for his bro.

He had a feeling it was Big Zone who did it because he had been laying low for a few weeks.

Tae cursed himself for not killing Big Zone when he had the chance to, but he knew his chance would come again soon.

It didn't take too long for him to get to the hospital. When Justin's sister called crying, he was about to link up with Winny.

When Winny called him to get up to chill, he was pumped up because when he saw how good she was looking, he couldn't resist.

Rena was out in Miami for the weekend with her cousins for their birthday, so he had some time to do him for a few days.

Tae cherished Rena and never cheated on her because there was no reason to. Her pussy was fire, and she was everything a nigga wanted.

In the hospital, the first person he saw was Ariel's skinny, cute dark-skinned ass sitting there with three of her friends.

"Tae!" Ariel jumped up, seeing her brother's best friend that she had a big crush on since a little girl.

"He's good?" Tae asked as she hugged him tightly.

"Yeah, the doctor said he just made it in the nick of time," Ariel said, wiping her tears.

"Good," Tae responded.

"Nobody can see him yet," Ariel told him.

"Iight. I'ma be back first thing in the morning, but I'ma leave dem here with you." Tae nodded to three of his goons.

"Ok."

Tae left with three men and went out to hunt down Big Zone or anybody close to him.

***

Northside, Raleigh

Lil Flex and his boys pulled into his projects they called NBA, and he was the leader, of course.

"He should be done in a few days. When shit die down, we will pull up on that Tae nigga," Lil Flex told his crew before walking to his baby mother's crib across the street.

Lil Flex was a short cocky nigga with long dreads and a little man complex, but he was an official street nigga.

He worked for Big Zone, so when his boss told him about the issue with Tae and Justin, he knew what needed to be done. Lil Flex and Justin were in the same Blood gang, but that didn't matter when it came to money.

It would be nice to kill Tae and Justin, then take over North Raleigh because they were making big money over there.

Lil Flex's baby mother was one of the baddest bitches in his hood, but the only thing was she had herpes and so did he. That's why he couldn't leave her alone, because she scared him for life.

Chapter 38
N.C. State University

Bri was sitting in her dorm room on her bed counting stacks of money, mostly all hundreds.

In a two-week time period, she made close to 175,000 on campus. She couldn't believe it. With a new car and an apartment near the school grounds, she was on top.

Bri set up a nice little operation where whoever wanted coke had to cop $100 worth or better and pills $200 or better. She would go to her customers' dorm rooms with beers or food, so she wouldn't look like a suspect.

The dorm hallways had a camera at each end of the hall because two years ago a student was murdered by another student in the school hall.

Her roommate was out of town at her dad's house, so she had the room to herself. After counting up the 16,700 dollars, she hid the money in her Louis Vuitton then opened up her drawer to see a black dildo 12 inch vibrator she rarely used.

Even though Bri had a recent boyfriend, she wasn't giving up no pussy yet. It was one of her rules.

Bri laid in her bed and spread her legs out, lifting her long white 2 Pac T-shirt, and then she moved her soaked pink panties to the side.

She rubbed the plastic dick on her swollen clit.

"Mmmmm," she moaned, easing the tip in her warm thin slit.

As she went deeper, her extra tight coochie wouldn't allow the toy to go further until she worked her way inside of her. She looked to her left and saw a good book by an author by the name of Romell Tukes called "Gangland Cartel" but his picture on the back caught her attention as she thought about him as she fucked herself harder.

"Ohhh yessss!" she yelled, looking at Romell Tukes' picture on the back of the book before she squirted all over the room. Her cum shot up in the air like a waterfall.

She felt like a creep masturbating off a man she didn't even know, but her roommate talked about how good his books were.

Bri's phone started to ring off the hook. Her customers needed their fix, so she cleaned up and got in the shower.

***

Weight County, N.C.

M.I. had a nice crib on the outside of Durham, but he had other spots also.

YN was in the living room area drinking since he arrived five minutes ago, but he walked in and didn't say a word. M.I. just looked up at him.

"Why you ain't answer my calls? Your phone was off," M.I. stated, seeing something was off with his little brother.

"We got a big problem," YN said in deep serious thought.

"That's why I was calling you because I'm hearing your boy Dusty is working for dem people," M.I. stated.

"How did you know?"

"So you knew about this shit the whole time, my nigga?" M.I. asked, knowing YN wouldn't keep such a secret so big from him.

"I just saw him speaking to a cop at a gas station," YN said.

"Damn, he's bold." M.I. knew it was official now.

"I'll take care of it."

"I know you will, and soon." M.I. got up to get dressed, so he could leave. YN sat in the living room plotting.

***

Downtown, Raleigh

Hustle had been so busy lately he had no family time, so he had to stop what he was doing so he could spend time with his beautiful daughter Rena.

"You used to love Ruth's Chris, babygirl," Hustle said to his daughter as they enjoyed their meal together.

"That was years ago," Rena said.

"No, that was a few months ago," Hustle said.

"You getting old." She laughed, realizing he'd been forgetting a lot of shit, but she knew that comes with age.

"How's your mom?" Hustle asked with a careless tone, and Rena always caught on to it. Her mom and dad hated each other for so many reasons and one was her mom was a cop, so she really hated his lifestyle.

When Hustle first met Rena's mom, he told her he was a businessman, but when she found out different, it was too late. Rena was born.

She felt like Hustle was a liar and a worthless piece of shit, the same thing she thought about all drug dealers.

"She good."

"Still a cop, huh?"

"Yeah, you know her," Rena shot back eating dinner, seeing a text from Tae. She wondered if it was the right time to tell her dad about Tae.

"How's work?"

"Hard, but I love it."

"Good, I'm proud of you, babygirl."

"Thank you."

"You got a boyfriend?" Hustle popped the question that caught her off guard.

"Who me?" Rena played dumb.

"You heard me."

"I do. His name is Tae, and I really like him. He treats me good, and I want you to meet him."

"It's that serious?"

"Yes," she said, smiling just thinking about him.

"Next time we get together, bring him along," Hustle told her.

They laughed, talked, ate, and enjoyed the night.

***

Raleigh, N.C.

Tae was chilling at his mom's crib, waiting for her to get off work, so he could take her out for her birthday.

He still couldn't believe his Uncle Will wanted his girlfriend dead. Rena, being a plug's daughter, was something he couldn't piece together because he saw no hood shit in her. She reminded him of one of those black chicks raised in a white upscale area with all white friends.

Tae did his own research on Hustle from an old nigga in his hood.

Tae found out Hustle was nothing to fuck with and his brother Chess when Tae asked the OG about Chess he told Tae some nigga named Will killed Chess. Well, that was the rumor in the street.

It was starting to make sense to Tae, how his uncle had been trying to use him as a puppet while he mastered the strings, but Tae was far from slow. He had been coming up with his own plan as well.

***

Downtown, Raleigh

Agent Moore's boss, Mr. Folker was looking over the death report of Agent Moore and his wife, who were found a few miles apart last month.

Looking at the crime scenes, he wondered how his agent could be caught up in some serious shit like that because Moore was a good guy. It was his whore wife that he disliked. Mr. Folker thought Kim had something to do with the agent's death, and he was going to do everything in order to find Moore's killer.

Closing the folder to the case, he looked outside his office window and then turned on his computer. When he saw the coast was clear, he watched porn with minors performing sexual acts. Mr. Folker had an addiction to child pornography and touching on them. He knew he needed help. At times, he wanted to kill himself because of his creepy addiction, but he just couldn't bring himself to do it.

Romell Tukes

Chapter 39
Downtown, Raleigh

Today, Justin was scheduled to be released from the hospital. He was feeling much better than a week ago when Lil Flex and his soldiers caught him slipping. The bullets punctured a lung and hit a kidney, but he was still alive, so he had to count his blessings.

His whole time there, his sister Ariel and Tae were there for him, and a few niggas from the block showed their love and concern by staying up there night and day to make sure he was protected.

"You ready?" Ariel walked in the room.

"We can leave now?" Justin leaned up on his shit bag.

"Nah in a few hours the people said, but I don't think we should go back to the hood. Let's go to Auntie's house in South Point." Ariel had her sleeping bag that she had been using for the past week in and out of the hospital.

"You know I don't fuck with Aunt Bella like that, Ariel."

"I know, but I told her we were coming and going, period," Ariel said, taking charge.

"Look at you all bossy."

"I'm not bossy. I'm just smarter than you because why would you want to go back to the hood right now, anyway. You know how your flashes are," Ariel told him.

"That's the gang. You feel me?"

"I don't. All I know is the gang got my brother wearing a shit bag with bullet holes in him." Ariel had to keep it real with Justin because nobody else would. His homies were too scared of him.

"Iight. I ain't finna argue with your young ass, and you need to put on some clothes."

"You can't argue with the truth, and these are shorts."

"Your ass hanging out the bottom."

"Mind your business. I'm grown now," Ariel said, walking out of the room to answer her phone call from her boyfriend.

***

North Raleigh, N.C.

"She's about to leave the hospital now, Lil Flex," Wee Wee said, who was one of Lil Flex's workers, but he was also Ariel's boyfriend. Wee Wee heard his big homie wanted to make sure Justin was dead. He informed him that he had been fucking his sister Ariel. Wee Wee wanted to prove his loyalty to the older niggas in the crew, especially Lil Flex.

"Iight. Bru, look. Wee Wee, Bat, and Gips all coming with me. We about to slide on this nigga," Lil Flex said inside the trap in NBA.

"What about Ariel?" Wee Wee didn't want his girl in the middle because he really liked her.

"Nigga, she can get it too. You got a problem wit that, bruh?" Lil Flex stated as everybody in the room looked at Wee Wee.

"Nah I'm down just asking, blood." Wee Wee corrected himself.

"Strap up. We sliding in two minutes." Lil Flex went to the back room to grab his favorite assault rifle AK-47.

After everybody strapped up, they walked outside to a black Ford Focus that they had been using to do drive-bys in and shoot outs.

When everybody got inside, Lil Flex saw Wee Wee sweating bullets when he was about to say something. That's when he saw the drop on him from outside his window.

Tat, Tat, Tat, Tat, Tat, Tat, Tat, Tat, Tat …

Five gunmen lit up the car, hitting everybody inside, including Lil Flex with a headshot, and Wee Wee was hit in the face seven times.

The rapid gun fire lasted thirty seconds. There were all types of assault rifle shell casings out on the ground, over sixty.

Tae and his crew hopped in their two SUVs parked across the street and got away.

***

Raleigh, N.C.

On the outskirts of the city, Rena and Tae got a little two-bedroom apartment together a few weeks ago. Tae let Rena hook it up. Tae had just come back from his mission. He walked in his house, hearing slow jams come from the bedroom. Walking into the room, he saw Rena laying on the bed butt ass naked. His penis instantly jumped up.

"Come here, Daddy," she said in a seductive way.

Tae quickly strapped down, not trying to play no games. She walked up to him, giving Tae a deep kiss then broke it off, guiding him to the king size bed. She laid on her back, revealing her nicely trimmed pretty pussy.

"Lick me," she said as he got between her legs and licked and sucked her pussy, which was already dripping wet.

"Fuck me." She couldn't take it no more. The fire and desire was all in her eyes.

Tae followed her order as he entered her slit, making her gasp as she tried to move her hips forward, letting his pipe slip into her inch by inch, fitting her perfectly.

"Ugghhh," she moaned, loving every inch of it.

"You want my dick?" he asked, running in and out of her at a steady pace. Feeling her pussy grip his cock almost made him shoot off.

Rena stopped him before he shot his load. She placed her lips on his rod and sucked his shaft like a mad woman until he came all in her mouth and she wanted more.

Tae bent her over and started fucking her doggy style with swift strokes, burying his big cock in her.

"Oh my God!" she screamed.

Tae fucked her silly like there was no tomorrow until they both reached a climax.

"What has gotten into you today? You never put it down like that." She collapsed on the side of him.

"One of them days."

"I have a question. Do you really love me?" Tae asked, because he was about to risk a lot for her.

"Yes, with my soul. Why?"

"Just asking."

"Well, don't ask shit you already know. I want you to meet my dad next week. He's really cool, Tae."

"Ok, I'll meet him, but when?"

"In a few days when I'm off. I got to set it up. I just want it to be perfect, baby."

"Ok. I'm with you, baby," Tae said, not knowing if he was ready to meet the man his uncle wanted dead. Tae didn't know if he should put Rena on game about her safety being at risk. He didn't want to scare her. He knew what needed to be done.

"I feel like everything in my life is perfect now," she said before closing her eyes to go to sleep.

Tae laid there looking at the ceiling, thinking about his next move and how he was going to stay two steps ahead of the game.

Chapter 40
North Raleigh, N.C.

Today was payday and Tae was running up money from a few of his traps, so he could re-up tonight when he saw his Uncle Will.

Business was going good, so he had been happy about that, but rumors had been going around about Glass' brother named Rags, putting a hit out on him and Justin from a jail cell.

Tae knew robbing and killing niggas for his uncle would soon catch up with him in the worst way, but he had no choice but to be ready for whatever.

That weekend, Rena wanted him to meet her dad, and he agreed to come along with her, but he wondered what would happen if her dad found out who he really was. Tae didn't have a back-up plan if shit went wrong, but he did know he loved Rena and wouldn't cross her for nothing.

Rena was out getting her gun license that day because he convinced her to. He explained that it was a crazy world and people were being killed left and right in the city.

Tae had to put the money up that he had on him in his safe house because riding around with two hundred thousand in cash wasn't smart with no paper trail.

The stash building was to his left, next to a tire shop that had been shut down for a decade now. Tae was thinking about re-opening it.

Bri was texting him all day, letting him know she was ready to see him again. Tae knew his sister was moving too fast, but he respected her grind. The truth was Bri was moving more product than any niggas he knew in the streets.

Justin was out of the way in the cut at his auntie's house healing up.

He walked into his apartment and rushed to the kitchen, where his stash spot was under the sink to place the money.

Tae heard a little squeak behind him and looked over his shoulder to see nothing. He was in a rush, so he tossed the money next to three other bags full of money.

Closing the cabinet over the sink, he was surprised to see a gun aimed at him by a masked man dressed in all black. Tae saw the hallway closet door wide open. The man had been hiding in the closet the whole time.

Tae cursed himself for not checking the crib when he entered, like he normally did.

"Handle your shit, bruh," Tae said, showing no fear whatsoever. Tae knew the game and death was the last phase of it, so he guessed today was his day.

The masked man looked at Tae sideways before pulling off his mask and lowering his weapon to his side.

Looking at who it was, Tae was shocked because he saw the man a few times and knew who he was.

"Your Uncle Will sent me to kill you, but I'm not," Spin told him.

"Why?"

"Will is a snake. He's been using you from the jump. I know damn well if he would snake his own blood and family snaking me would be like taking candy from a toddler," Spin uttered.

"Damn, he tried to do a nigga like that, bruh?" Tae was stunned as he leaned on the kitchen counter.

"Don't act surprised. You ain't see this shit coming?" Spin laughed.

"Of course. Just not so fast, cuz."

"I came to warn you, bruh. Maybe we can come together and put something in motion because he finna keep trying to get at you." Spin was honest with him.

"Ok, give me a few days," Tae said as he saw Bri calling him.

"Be safe." Spin left. He knew when Will found out that Tae was still alive, he would throw a fit.

Spin didn't give a fuck. He planned to tell Will he didn't see Tae yet. Will knew about Tae's stash house. He told Spin he could catch Tae there today before he met him to re-up.

***

Coke Boys

A few minutes ago, Tae called Will, informing him that he was ready to meet. Will couldn't believe he was still alive because Spin was supposed to take him out earlier.

Will called Spin to find out why Tae was still alive, but his phone went to voicemail. He was pissed off.

Waiting outside of a fast food spot, he brought Bank with him just in case Tae knew something.

"There he go," Will said, seeing a Hellcat fly into the parking lot, making Will nervous. He saw Tae get out with a big bag. He knew money was in the duffle bag.

Will got out of the Maybach and got himself together, hiding his fear and nervousness.

"Nephew!" Will shouted, showing a fake smile.

"My favorite uncle. Where you been at?" Tae asked, giving him a hug while handing him the duffle bag.

"Laying low. Good to see you." Will dropped his head.

"That's everything."

"I'ma have that to you in a few days," Will said.

"Nah, I need that shit tonight. I'ma be going out of town soon, so I need you to bust that move for me," Tate told him.

"Ok, sure. I got'cha."

"Money on the wood, make da game go good. You taught me that. Fair exchange is no robbery." Tae looked at Will with a bright smile.

"True."

"Hit me in an hour or so. My goons are waiting," Tae said.

"What's been going on with Big Zone?" Will asked, almost forgetting.

"Ask him, bruh. I got my goons on it, but I'm sure you can move a lot faster when you want something done," Tae said before walking off.

Will thought hard on what he heard just now and then walked to his car, not wanting to overlook it. When he got in the car, Bank shook his head with a chuckle.

Chapter 41
Wake Forest County, N.C.

Hustle had a lavish mansion on the outskirts of Raleigh, N.C. It was 10,762 square ft., five bedrooms, four bathrooms, a guest room, four car garage, and a large outback area.

Tae and Rena arrived at her father's estate in her Benz dressed nicely, and so was Tae in slacks and a button up.

"You look nervous, baby." Rena looked at him, seeing he was a little uncomfortable.

"I'm past nervous."

"I told you, bae. You don't have to be. My pops is cool. You will like him, trust me. This is the first time I brought any man to his house, so he knows I'm serious about you," Rena told him before getting out of the car with her lime-green Chanel bag that matched her Ralph & Russo dress.

"Iight." Tae admired the house and saw a Bentley truck, and a few other luxury cars parked outside.

There was a beautiful dark-skinned woman with long legs and the thickest curves Tae had ever seen on a woman. She had a flat stomach. Tae couldn't help but stare at one of the baddest females he had ever seen in his life. He thought the lady was Rena's sister.

"Rena," the woman said, smiling and hugging Rena.

"Hey, Anna."

"Oh my gosh. I haven't seen you in months. When your father told me you and your boyfriend were coming over for dinner, I had to prepare your favorite meal," Anna stated, referring to curry and jerk chicken. Rena loved Caribbean food. It was a part of her culture because she had some West Indian in her blood.

"Thanks. This is my hubby. His name is Tae," she introduced.

"Hey, Tae. I'm Anna. I'm Harold's girlfriend," she replied.

"Nice to meet you." Tae saw the woman had exotic blue eyes. He was fucked up by that.

"Come on in. Your dad is waiting in the dining room watching football. I'ma finish up dinner," Anna said, walking off as her booty clapped all over the place in a pair of leggings.

***

Hustle was sitting watching the football game when he heard the commotion. He knew who it was.

"Daddy." Rena hugged Hustle tightly as he peeped over his shoulder, looking at Tae.

"Hey, babygirl. You on time. You look beautiful," Hustle stated.

"Thanks."

"Who's this? The Tae kid?" Hustle asked as he was standing up.

"Yes, dad. This is my boyfriend, Tae, I been telling you about." Rena gave her dad a look, letting him know to be good.

"How are you doing?" Hustle gave Tae a firm handshake, looking him in his eyes.

"Nice to finally meet you. Rena speaks highly of you, sir," Tae stated.

"She should. You have an amazing young lady here. They don't make them like her no more," Hustle said, making Rena blush.

"I'ma go help Anna with dinner. Y'all behave, okay? Daddy, please be nice," Rena said with a serious face, letting him know she meant business.

"You raised a good woman," Tae said, sitting down.

"Let's cut the bullshit. What the fuck you want with my baby if you work for Will? Why you ain't killed her because I know your uncle wanted you to." Hustle was straight forward.

"I'm my own man and would never bring harm to her. I truly love her," Tae said, a little caught off guard by his comment.

"If you even think about harming my baby, I will come for your whole family. I know who you are and everything about you," Hustle said.

"You can do whatever, but I will never bring harm to a person I love," Tae said seriously.

"I hope so ..." Hustle saw Rena walk out with a tray of food.

"Dinner is ready. What y'all talking about?" Rena asked.

"Your dad and I like the same football team," Tae said.

"Go Jaguars," Hustle added.

"I told you both y'all would like each other." Rena went back into the kitchen.

"We'll finish up the convo one day, but I'ma tell you this: keep your eyes on your uncle. Some men aren't to be trusted, and he is one of them," Hustle said.

"I know," Tae said as the women started coming out with food so they could enjoy their meal together. The meal was successful and Rena couldn't have been happier the way the night turned out.

Rena knew Hustle liked Tae because he pulled her to the side and told her so, that confirmed it.

***

Durham, N.C.

Betty came home from school early today and her mom was in the kitchen cooking dinner for them tonight. Main her brother hadn't been around in a few days, so Betty was getting high off the weed a kid in her school gave her.

Her mom never came in her room, so she was good. Smoking was something she liked to do when she felt lonely and depressed. Two months ago, Betty's bestfriend committed suicide in her house when Betty went to use the bathroom.

Betty's friend slit both of her wrists. By the time help came, it was too late. Her bestie used to tell Betty how her father raped her and beat on her mom every day. Her bestfriend used to say things like she would rather be dead than to continue to live the life she was used to.

Locking her bedroom door, she went into her stash spot and pulled out a pre-rolled blunt she had been craving all day since her second period class.

She turned up the Ella Mai album that she loved to death and lit the blunt, laying back on her loveseat. She took off her school uniform and laid there in bra and panties, admiring her C-cup breasts and nice toned thighs. A lot of older dudes thought she was much older than 16 when they tried to bag her.

Betty was so high when she was done smoking, she fell asleep with the blunt stuck in between her fingers as the fire went out.

All of a sudden, Betty thought she heard gun fire. She jumped up, thinking she was tripping, but when she heard the loud noise again, she rushed to turn off the music. Seconds later, her door was kicked open.

"Ahhhhhhhh…" she screamed as three men rushed her, pinning her to the floor, covering her mouth while ripping off her bra and panties.

One of the men started to rape her. She bit his hand but that only led to a punch to her face, almost knocking her out.

"Uhmm, noo. Please stop. You're hurting me," Betty cried, unable to handle the man's penis. After he nutted in her pussy, another one bent Betty over while another man held her hands, waiting on his turn.

When she felt the cock ram into her tiny asshole, she flew forward, but was blocked with another dick to her face. The next man made her suck his cock. After an hour of raping her, YN walked in telling them the party was over, and he shot Main's little sister in the head. They left her mom slumped on the kitchen floor in a pool of blood with fried chicken and hot grease all over her body, which cause third- degree burns.

Chapter 42
Atlanta, GA

Tae and Justin took a flight to Atlanta for the All-Star weekend to get out of the city for a few days.

"That baby almost threw up all over my Prada shoes that was on the side of us, bru," Justin said, looking at his red and black kicks.

"Nigga, I told you not to sit so close, goofy," Tae said as they waited on the luggage to come through the machine.

"I thought we were flying first class?"

"It was booked. I lied so you would come," Tae said, seeing their bags.

"I bet, but that shit crazy, bru. I can't believe ole girl's pops is that nigga Hustle," Justin stated.

"Fuck that, I can't believe Will had the fucking nerve to send a hit on me even though I eventually saw it coming," Tae admitted.

"We got this Big Zone nigga to worry about, and now Rags," Justin added, knowing shit wasn't about to get better.

"I know we need to find a new plug soon because this may have been my last shipment from Will," Tae said.

The last time he saw Will and gave him the money for his re-up, Tae had his goons follow Will around even to his wife's crib until he got his product just in case any games were being played. Tae saw how scared Will was, seeing him alive and well.

"Your girl's dad?" Justin threw out there while they walked out of the airport to the Uber.

"Damn, why I ain't think of that?" Tae questioned.

"Maybe because that's your Uncle Will's enemy," Justin told him, being funny.

"I'ma wait for the right time," Tae said.

"Fuck all dat Cordina shit tonight. Let's go shopping and then hit up some clubs, my nigga."

"I'm down," Tae replied.

They hit up the mall and went sight-seeing in the city before going back to their hotels to prepare for the club later that night.

***

Blue Flame Strip Club, ATL

Justin was vibing with a bad ass dancer all night. It got so real that he gave her a band just to spend an hour with him in a private section.

The woman told him she was in college and needed the extra money, so she would come hit the club twice or three times a week.

Justin never met a woman so smart and sexy with class. He didn't judge her for what she did because that was sucker shit, but he respected her mind frame while the goofies only saw her as a body part.

"I see something in you, Justin. Your aura is different. I don't even respect these niggas up in here all thirsty with a wife at home blowing their rent money," Olivia stated making him laugh hard, but he still felt pain from being shot and she peeped it.

"That's real."

"Facts but I don't want your money. I sat here with you and you not one time asked me for a dance, sexual favors, or asked me to degrade myself," Olivia said.

"That's just me, Olivia."

"Well, I like you. Please don't change."

"I won't," Justin told her. "I get off in thirty minutes. You wanna grab a bite to eat?" she asked.

"You treating?"

"Maybe just maybe," she said, getting up and walking away and making her ass jiggle, giving him a good look at her gap.

"Damn, my nigga. Who dat?" Tae asked as he walked back into the section with a pocket full of ones and a bottle of Moet.

"She cool, bro. She about to take us out to eat," Justin said.

"You cuffing dancers?" Tae joked.

"Nah, we just vibing."

"The strip club ain't meant to catch a vibe," Tae told him.

"Whatever, bro. I ain't fucking with you right now," Justin told him looking on stage to see bitches playing with their pussies.

The rest of the night was fun. They went to a 24/7 food spot, talked and had a good time. Justin and Olivia both went back to the hotel room and talked until dawn.

***

Durham, N.C.
Two weeks later

Main had to bury his sister and mom today. This was one of the worst days of his life. Scrilla and the 700 gang were sitting to his left like the Mafia, showing support to their homie Main.

When Main got the news of his family being killed, it touched his heart and led him into a deep depression that had him considering committing suicide. Several times, he put a gun to his own head but didn't pull the trigger.

At the hospital, Main found out that his little sister was raped. He knew muthafuckers were sick in the head to rape and kill a little girl.

After today, Main told himself that he would put his heart on ice. He knew there was no coming back after burying his loved ones.

Tears flowed down his face as close to 300 people came out to mourn.

Main hadn't said a word in days to anybody. Those close to him knew it would take a while for him to get his mind right, but those that knew him well understood that he would eventually go on a killing spree to extract revenge.

Romell Tukes

Chapter 43
Durham, N.C.

Dayman Carts Apartments was a nice, low-key apartment complex area in a middle-class neighborhood.

Ronny had just got off work from the same job he had been working on for over two decades now, and he hated it. Spending ten to twelve hours a day in a metal factory wasn't his dream growing up as a kid.

Ronny's biological dad, brothers, and uncles were the biggest dope dealers in Durham when he was growing up, but he chose pimping as a different route.

Becoming a pimp was something that was not in his blood at first, but he was so into the pimp game that it became a part of his blood, and it spilled over to his son M.I.

When he was married to M.I.'s mom, she was his bottom whore but when she got a real job shit changed. The biggest pimp in Durham retired and started working for the police to save his own ass.

A big case was about to rain on Ronny, so he snitched on his dad and two of his brothers, getting them both over 100 years in prison.

Ronny then started working at a metal factory and broke up with M.I.'s mom.

Now Ronny was re-married to a nice black woman from Chicago. Ronny recently ratted on his birth son, but thinking he had his reasons, and one reason was because he disliked drug dealers.

Ronny wanted to help the police clean up the streets of Durham, and he knew his son was the main source in the city, so he knew he had to start with him.

He got out of his car and walked into his house.

"Erica!" Ronny yelled to hear nothing at all, which was odd.

Ronny walked deeper into the crib to hear the sink water running in the kitchen.

"Baby, I'm home. I had a long day," Ronny said, putting his bag down to see his wife's body laid out on the floor in a pool of blood.

Ronny was so shocked he caught cold feet as if he was stuck to the ground.

"This is the outcome of your flaws. Ratting is like a one way trip to hell. I knew you was a bitch nigga when you left my mom because she needed help. That's why I bought her a salon," M.I. stated, standing up with a Glock 17 in his hand, stepping over the blood spill.

"Son, please," Ronny cried.

"Don't call me son. Please, you not even my stepdad."

"How can I make this right? I don't even know what's going on," Ronny played dumb as M.I. laughed.

"You had the balls to snitch on your own son."

"M.I. you were killing our black people, I couldn't let you keep poisoning our people," Ronny said backing up into the counter.

"What the fuck you talking about, bro. You putting black people in prison, so don't act like you're a fucking activist now, bitch ass nigga!" M.I. shouted.

Ronny didn't say a word because he knew M.I. was right.

"I ..."

Bloc...

Bloc...

Bloc...

Bloc...

M.I. shot Ronny in the face twice and two times in the chest, knocking him off his feet, then standing over him and firing two more shots into Ronny's body.

He walked out of the crib without any type of remorse at all. M.I. hated rats, but he embraced snakes.

***

Downtown, Raleigh

Big Zone was on his way to pick up his sister Winny from her six month checkup she went to when it was time.

He had been laying low spending family time with family since the FEDS and the DEA had been hitting his spots all over the city. Big Zone knew there was a rat in his circle, but he just couldn't find the missing link.

Lil Flex was gone, so now he only had a few soldiers he could count on to hold shit down. Big Zone partly blamed himself because he knew this was all Will's work. He was letting an old sucker destroy his empire.

Big Zone planned to get at a nigga he knew from way back to see if he could help him make some sense of this all. His boy M.I. lived in Durham, and he planned to pay him a visit soon.

Parking in front of the clinic, he waited for Winny to come out.

***

Winny stood there waiting on the lady who gave her the STD test results to write out the type of meds she would need to cure her three STDs she received from her new boyfriend, Tip.

Winny tried her best not to cry as she cursed herself for not wearing condoms with Tip. She got a text from Big Zone saying he was outside. There was no way she could tell her brother about this because he would really kill Tip.

"Here's your medicine prescriptions that you will need to get better," the doctor said, feeling sorry for Winny because she was so beautiful.

"Thanks," Winny replied, placing the prescriptions in her purse. She checked the time on the wall, rushing out of the doctor's office with her head down, feeling embarrassed.

Big Zone was standing on the sidewalk, talking on the phone next to the luxury car. Winny looked to her left and saw two men rushing across the street with guns, and she recognized them both.

Winny saw Tae and Justin about to get the drop on her brother, so she did the only thing she could think of, which was to yell.

"Zack!" she shouted Big Zone's government name out, getting his attention.

Big Zone was about to turn around to see what Winny wanted as she called his name out loud.

Seeing the two shooters, he turned and started running the opposite way as gun blasting filled the streets.

The civilians that were out immediately ran in buildings or took cover somewhere low to avoid being killed.

Big Zone jumped over a body making a left into a garage's parking lot, leaving Winny behind. Big Zone didn't know that Winny was shot four times when the gun fire started.

***

Tae ran back to the car with Justin to get away after missing their target, but Tae couldn't believe he just shot Winny.

"You saw her?" Tae asked, driving off, hearing sirens in the opposite direction.

"Winny?" Justin saw her too, but he hoped it wasn't her.

"Wrong place, wrong time," Tae said, a little saddened because Winny was a good chick. He recently saw her on social media happily hugged up with her boyfriend.

"Guess it's life, but that big nigga took flight."

"We will get him," Tae said.

Chapter 44
Downtown, Raleigh

Rena had been on her high horse for the past few days because everything had been going so good, at work, her love life, and her family was good. Growing up, she learned how to be very family oriented.

One day, she wanted to have kids and a big family to live on with her legacy. Meeting a man like Tae was unheard of nowadays because mostly all of the men were cheaters, liars, broke, bums, and had no ambition.

Luckily, Tae was the opposite of everything she disliked in men.

Today, she had to stay at work a little later than usual to do some files and shit for her boss.

When it hit 8 p.m., she finished up and got her things together to go home to Tae and give him some good loving.

Exiting the office, she saw how dark it was outside, and she saw a van circling the lot, but she paid it no mind.

Her phone rang, and she saw it was her father calling her, so she answered.

"Daddy." She put Hustle on speaker.

"What you doing baby?" Hustle asked.

"I'm great. Just leaving work on my way back home. You ready for our double date this weekend?" she asked, unaware that the van crept a few inches up behind her.

"That sounds cool," Hustle said.

Rena heard a van door slide open and looked back to see four men jump out and rush her.

"Nooooo …" Rena screamed, dropping her phone on the floor, leaving her dad on speaker as she tried to fight her way out of the ambush, but that only worsened her situation. The kidnappers started beating her up as if she was a nigga.

A Hellcat wide body raced through the lot and ran into one of the kidnappers. Tae jumped out with a Mack 10 submachine gun.

Tat…

Tat…

Tat…

Tat…

Tat…

Tat…

Tat…

Tae shot all of them except the driver, who pulled off wanting no smoke. One kidnapper was still moving, but he was crawling to get away, but Tae ran down on him.

"Will sent us, man. I'm sorry we wasn't gonna kill her." The man on the floor said, trying to slide away on his buttocks.

Tae squeezed the trigger, emptying the rest of the rounds into the last man's body.

Rena was using Tae's car to get back up, feeling lightheaded and dizzy from the power blows she received from the men.

"You ok?" Tae asked Rena, helping her straighten up, seeing she had two black eyes, a swollen face, and a busted mouth.

"I got a big headache," she said, feeling something was terribly wrong with her head.

"We going to a hospital outside of Raleigh." Tae saw her phone on the floor and picked it up before putting Rena in the car. Tae did not know her phone was on the whole time until he passed it to Rena.

"I'm ok, dad."

"Where are you at?" Hustle yelled into the phone, as he had been doing since he heard the commotion.

"I'm on my way to the hospital. Meet us at Duke Hospital," Rena said before her phone died.

"Lean back and relax," Tae told her, hopping on the highway.

"Tae, what is going on and who is Will?" Rena asked, her head spinning.

Tae knew it was time to be honest with her, because he hated hiding shit from her.

"People want you dead because of your father, and they wanted me to kill you first, but when I saw it was you I didn't do it, then they tried to kill me," Tae told her.

"What?" She couldn't believe her ears.

"I'm sorry, but it's my Uncle Will. He's at war with Hustle and me now."

"You knew my dad was Hustle the whole time?"

"Yes."

"I should have told you, but I didn't want to scare you or push you away," she replied.

"It's ok, just lay back, and chill," Tae said doing 95 mph down the expressway.

"I really love you, Tae. You saved my life." Rena knew he was the one she was meant to spend the rest of her life with.

***

Duke Hospital, Durham

At the hospital, Rena was seen quickly, but Tae had to wait in the front until she was done.

Hustle walked with six big black gorilla looking guards.

"Where is she?" Hustle asked Tae, approaching him upset.

"She okay, the doctors are running tests on her, but she good. When I got there, they was trying to kidnap her and ended up hitting her. They fucked her up pretty bad, but I took care of them," Tae assured him as Hustle stared in his eyes.

"Walk with me," Hustle said, walking off down the hall.

"I took care of it. You have my word as I told you I love her."

"How did you know they were going to be there for my daughter?" Hustle asked.

"Will wanted me to kill her, but when I found out who it was, I couldn't do it. Then he tried to kill me. After that, I kept a close eye on Rena at work because I knew he had her work place info because he gave it to me. I was on point, that's all," Tae stated, seeing Hustle nod his head.

"You did good, but I want you to come to my house alone this weekend. I have to go. I can't see my daughter all bruised up. You better get to your uncle before I do because he is the only man who would have some balls to do this," Hustle said.

"That's not my uncle no more as far as I'm concerned, and I think it's the other way around because if I see him I'ma make him wish my grandmom swallowed him," Tae said, making Hustle smile.

"I got a famous quote for you by a man named Sun-Tzu," Hustle said, seeing his goons crack their knuckles ready to put in some work.

"I heard of Sun-Tzu." Tae heard of him back in the day.

He stated, "Put them in a spot where they have no place to go, and they will die before fleeing. That's from him, so I advise you to take that and run with it. I'll see you on Saturday," Hustle said, leaving out of the hospital.

Tae soaked up all the game Hustle just dropped on him. Two hours later, the doctor came out and told Tae that Rena had a minor blood clot in her head and would need to stay 24 hours, so they could make sure she was good, and it wouldn't increase because it could get dangerous.

Tae wanted to be there all night with Rena because he knew she would do it for him. He felt bad that all of that happened to her..

Chapter 45
Raleigh, N.C.

Big Zone and M.I. linked up with each other and met up at Jaycee Park. Both crews had a gang of niggas with them posted up in the car lot, while the two bosses walked around the park together, chopping it up.

"This been long overdue, dawg. You feel me?" M.I. said.

"I agree. We always cross paths out of town somewhere when we both was fucking with Will," Big Zone stated.

"True, but speaking of Will. That is the reason I asked you to come out today because I heard you're going through some issues out here too?" M.I. asked.

"You heard right, and I believe Will hoe ass stuck his wolves on me and ever since my city been a war zone, bruh." Big Zone shook his head.

"I lost a lot fucking with this nigga Will. It's like he's hiding out while he let his goons handle his work. I'm losing men, blocks, money, and patience." M.I. hadn't had any good sleep in a while since beefing with them little niggas from 700 Block.

"We gotta do something quick because this shit is getting out of pocket. If them little niggas know like I do, then Will won't take long before he uses them and cross them up as well, shawty. Trust me," Big Zone said.

"Habits are hard to break, bruh. I'm with you on that one," M.I. said.

"Give me a few. I'ma put a plan together. I gotta bury my sister first."

"Iight. Sorry about the lost, but we'll get back, cuz," M.I. stated, walking back to the car lot where his guards awaited him.

***

Southside, Durham
Meanwhile

In Fargo Apartments, Cee J and two of his soldiers had been cutting up heroin, which they called dog food in the city.

Everybody had on masks and gloves because the dope they were cutting was so strong it could get you high if you caught serious contact with it.

"How that bitch Anikka tried to charge me for the pussy last night?" Cee J stated to his boys.

"Ain't that your ex?" Bolt said in his Haitian accent.

"Yeah but I ain't fuck her in years, so when I saw her in the club she was looking different. The bitch got her body done and all dat, bru. Feel me?" Cee J stated.

"I saw her on Only Fans a few days ago on the internet. I paid to see that ass," Chris said, placing the tan powder substance in the small bags.

"Fuck that stank pussy bitch," Cee J added.

"So you know her shit stank and you was still trying to fuck?" Bolt asked.

"Hell, yeah. Her head game crazy," Cee J repeated before hearing a knock at the door.

"That maybe Shayniece," Bolt said, looking to see if his baby mama who lived there came back from work early.

"Scared ass nigga." Cee J laughed, knowing how scared Bolt was of his baby mama, who was bigger and taller than Bolt.

The door opened and shit got wicked in a matter of seconds.

BOOM...

BOOM...

BOOM...

BOOM...

BOOM...

Bolt's stomach was blown out of his back by the shotgun pump as niggas ran past him when his body slammed on the ground.

Cee J had a gun to his right on the table next to five keys of dope that he had planned to cut up today.

Boc, Boc, Boc, Boc, Boc, Boc, Boc ...

Cee J shot two niggas, giving one of the men a head shot.

Scrilla and Main ducked the bullets and popped up shooting, putting bullet holes all over the place and one in Cee J's chest. The shotgun blast knocked Cee J out of his chair.

BOOM...

BOOM...

When Main shot the last man, they raided the crib to find 200,000 in cash and a few keys of dog food in the back rooms.

Two of Scrilla's men were left dead on the floor near the doorway, but he knew there was nothing he could do about it.

Robbing niggas there would always be a chance someone wouldn't make it out.

***

North Carolina University, N.C.

Bri's boyfriend just left her dorm room after fucking the shit out of her. She was so tired and drained that she sat down on her couch, taking three deep breaths.

"God damn," she said, feeling how sore and swollen her coochie was. No nigga ever put it down on her like her boyfriend did. She never knew she could take 12 inches of pipe in her tight little walls, but she was doing her thing.

Money had been flowing crazy. She had so many clients. She needed workers, so she put her roommate and another chick on to some money. Bri had two phones booming all day long.

Her boyfriend also helped her from time to time but had his own thing going on, selling pounds of weed.

Tae was not answering his phone for two days, and she started to get a little worried because she knew how dangerous Raleigh could get.

Bri was seeing a lot of murders going on in Raleigh on the news and in the newspapers, so she was worried.

Romell Tukes

Chapter 46
Durham, N.C.

Scrilla was on his way to Tucker Street, so he could sell the keys to his boy Kold who was getting money off dog food for years.

Not eating anything all day long, Scrilla pulled over at a pizza shop to his left. He grabbed a slice of extra cheese pizza real quick to hold him over.

The crew was upset about two of their homies in the Cee J shoot out, but Scrilla explained to them that it was a part of the game.

Bank called him that morning, telling him that he would be in the city around 6 p.m. to speak to him. Scrilla agreed.

When he first met Bank, he liked his vibe and energy, but he still didn't trust him.

Scrilla parked on the curb and left his car running like gas was free. Walking inside, he saw Stacy coming out with a pregnant tummy. All types of thoughts flooded his head.

"Stacy," he said as she looked at him with wide eyes, as if something was wrong.

Before she could reply, her boyfriend and soon to be baby father came out of the pizza shop with a box of pizza.

When both men's eyes locked, they couldn't believe their luck. YN dropped the box of pizza and went for his weapon, but Scrilla was faster on his draw.

Bloc, Bloc, Bloc, Bloc, Bloc …

Scrilla hit Stacy in her temple and in her left shoulder blade before he ducked for cover.

YN saw Stacy's lifeless body and started busting off wild shots all over the place. YN and Stacy were a couple for two years. She was his wifey, but he didn't have a clue that she was a natural born cheater.

Boc, Boc, Boc, Boc, Boc, Boc, Boc, Boc, Boc…

A cop car bent the corner, speeding like a NASCAR driver.

Scrilla and YN both took off on foot, going in different directions as the cop jumped out of the cop car. The police officer was three hundred pounds and all fat. So chasing them was out the question. He called the shooting in, saw Stacy's dead pregnant body, and felt sad for her, but the white cop was more mad that he let the two suspects get away.

***

Wake County, N.C.

Agent Folker drove home trying to put everything together that he had been researching, and none of it made sense at all. What did make sense was the file he found of a snitch who had been working for the federal government for some time now.

He'd been working hard on the Agent Moore case and the murder of his wife a lot. Pulling into his driveway, he couldn't wait to get inside and settle down.

Off work, Mr. Folker lived a very private life that he didn't want anybody to know about.

Inside, he had six bolt locks on his front door. He rushed to his lower basement. His basement looked like a real live torture chamber. There were two little boys and two little girls sitting down in the two large built-in cages that he had installed when he first bought the house.

Mr. Folker kidnapped the kids a few months ago from other states by tricking them with candy and toys at parks and at school yard playgrounds.

"Hi, my babies. Who's coming to spend the night with daddy?" he asked, seeing the fear on all of their faces. Every night he would take one of the kids up to his bedroom, give them a shower, perform sexual acts on them, and cuddle with them until it was sunrise.

Mr. Folker always had a sick mind as a kid after being raped daily. He was too ashamed to tell somebody, so he bottled it in until it became a nasty, sick fetish and fantasy for him to torture kids the way he was.

"You come here," Mr. Folker pointed at a little Spanish boy who was ten years old. Everybody down there was nine through eleven years old, his lucky number.

When Mr. Folker saw that the kid didn't want to move, he grabbed his taser and opened the cage. Not wanting to be tased again, he got up and did what he was told.

"Better me than R. Kelly, or how about that scary Michael Jackson?" Mr. Folker laughed, closing the gate, going upstairs with a sick smile.

***

Raleigh, N.C.

Rena had been at home healing up and trying to recover, but she would not be going back to work any time soon, or at least until Tae told her she could.

Almost losing her life to a blood clot in her head, she felt blessed and had Tae's good timing to thank.

Her dad came by to check on her earlier that day to tell her that he didn't want her to leave the house. Hustle even tried to give her a gun just in case, but she already had a piece. She had her license and gun permit.

Tae was visiting his cousin, who was in jail. Her face still had a few bruises, but she didn't like sitting around the house all day doing nothing.

***

Raleigh County Jail, N.C.

Tae was on a visit with his cousin Low Dee, who just got sentenced to a fresh 12 years in jail.

Low Dee was pissed off about that, but he knew Allah put him in jail for a reason because he was in the streets wilding, killing, selling dope, and robbing niggas.

"You look more stressed than me, bru. I would do anything to be in your shoes right now," Low Dee stated.

"Fuck no you wouldn't, I got all types of niggas trying to kill me," Tae said.

"Like who?" Low Dee had no clue.

"Will put a hit on me, and he still thinks I don't know."

"I told you not to fuck with that nigga, dawg," Low Dee knew this was gonna happen.

"I knew, but he gave me a way and I took it. Now I'm about to meet wit Hustle tomorrow."

"Hold on, you know Hustle?" Low Dee asked, hearing his little cousin name big dawgs in the city.

"He's my girl's dad."

"Damn, he the real deal, but he hated Will. I hear good things about Hustle. I think you need to fuck with him. He's a millionaire. You're in the best position," Low Dee told his favorite cousin.

"I know in due time."

"If you finna play the game, gone, cuz. Play it like it's no tomorrow and play to win," Low Dee told him before their visit was almost down.

Chapter 47
Durham, N.C.

Scrilla checked the time in his car, seeing that he arrived at the W hotel on time downtown to meet up with Banks, who called him for the past few days.

Since the pizza shoot out with YN, Scrilla had been trying to lay low for a while. When he saw Stacy with YN, he knew he had to be her boyfriend that she always talked about. If Scrilla knew she was YN's girl, he would have killed them both.

He pulled up next to a black Impala with its headlights on, he figured that was Bank waiting on him.

Scrilla couldn't get the thought of killing a pregnant woman out of his head. That wasn't something he wanted to do on purpose.

Bank got out of the car in an all-black ninja outfit as if he was going on a night stalking mission.

"Scrilla, good to see you."

"What's good?" Scrilla wasn't really in the mood for small talk.

"I need your help," Bank said.

"My help? What are you getting at? I can't even help myself right now."

"Nah, bru. This type of help is gonna save your life," Bank said, seeing an awkward expression on Scrilla's face.

"I'm lost." Scrilla didn't have a clue what Bank was asking, but he started to wonder if he was playing games.

"I'm not who you think I am," Bank said.

"So who da fuck are you?"

"I'm a federal agent that's been undercover for some time now, building a big case on Will and Hustle," Bank said.

"What nigga, so what the fuck you want with me?" Scrilla shot back.

"I need your help. Will is going to kill you. I'm giving you a chance to take this fucker down, but there is only one issue I'm having. Will's cases keep coming up missing. He has somebody in high ranks looking out for him, but with your help, we can-" Bank was about to keep going until Scrilla cut him off.

"Nigga, WE nothing. I ain't no rat!" Scrilla shouted, upset that Bank even tried to play him for a rat.

"Save yourself, Scrilla."

"If I wanted to get saved, I would have went to church." Scrilla walked off.

Bank stood there watching the car Scrilla arrived in pull off. Bank was a crooked, dirty federal cop trying to build a case on Will himself. His supervisor was backing him a little, but not as much as he needed him to.

On the side, Bank was selling drugs in South Carolina, making a lot of money. He also wanted to get Will out of the way, so he could take over his operations. He came up with a smooth plan to get rid of Will, and he knew how to move his chess pieces on the board, starting with Scrilla.

When Bank walked around his car, shots rang out from the lot, and Bank went into action, busting back.

Boc, Boc, Boc, … Boom, Boom, Boom, Boom …

Bank waved bullets. While shooting back at the gunmen, he got a close-up on seeing Spin trying to kill him.

Boc, Boc, Boc, Boc, Boc …

Bank's gun jammed, and he tossed it. He climbed in his car and peeled off. Bullets continued to hit his car as he drove out of the lot trying to get to safety.

Seeing Spin try to kill him, he didn't know what that was about, but it was on and popping now.

***

Spin drove off in his ride on to his next mission. He was very mad that he missed his target. He'd been watching Bank for a few days to kill him.

When he saw him choppin it up with Scrilla, he could tell that whatever it was that Bank told Scrilla, he wasn't feeling it at all. Spin had no clue that Bank was the feds. He just wanted him out of his way.

Spin came up with a plan of success when he was in Greensboro, hiding out from the law.

The plan was supposed to go into effect tonight, but the first step was a fumble, so now he was on the way to Will's stash house in North Durham.

Robbing Will, then killing Bank would open up doors for him to lock down the city and send work to his cousins in Greensboro.

Will texted Spin early that morning telling him he would be at the stash house later, so Spin was on his way.

***

North Durham, N.C.

Spin drove down a street filled with nice middle-class houses in rows with nice manicured lawns.

Spin didn't see Will's car anywhere in sight. He cursed himself again because he wanted to kill him. He knew Bank would tell him what happened minutes ago. He was nervous.

Getting out of his car, he busted out the window on the side of the house, climbing in the window cutting up his hand.

Inside the lush home, he went to the safe in the bedroom to see it was open wide with a yellow letter inside.

"What the fuck is going on?" Spin said out loud to himself, picking up the letter to read it.

You young bitch ass nigga. I knew you was a snake when I first saw you. That's why I put you on the team, but you went wrong trying to snake me. I'ma king cobra. You're a garter snake. I'll see you soon, sucker ...

Romell Tukes

Chapter 48
Whitfield County, N.C.

Tae walked up to Hustle's door and rang the bell for their get together over a nice lunch. Tae didn't know what the meeting was going to be about, but he was ready. All he knew was he was going to stand his ground as a man.

Two big guards opened the door and searched Tae for wires and weapons. He had neither one. They let him inside and took him to the basement area.

When Tae entered the basement, he liked the way it looked down there. It was large and spacious.

The floor was designed like a chessboard with glass tables, a glass bar, and a pool table that was also glass. Tae could tell he spent some money on the basement area, but when he saw the glass chessboard and pieces everywhere, he knew Hustle was a chess player.

"Tae, welcome my future son-in-law. Would you like a drink?" Hustle asked in an all-white business suit.

"Sure, this is a nice set up."

"I know," Hustle shot back, pouring himself and Tae a drink.

"This room is special to me. As you see, everything is made out of glass and the whole room looks like a chessboard," Hustle said, bringing the drinks to the table.

"Why is that?" Tae wanted to know.

"The glass is a symbol of clarity in life. You have to learn how to see things from the good and the bad, but our insight has to be clear not foggy."

"That makes sense," Tae agreed.

"The chess logo is for my brother. He was my brother and father. His name was Chess, so when I'm down here I feel closer to him, and he was a chess master. That leads to my next question. Do you play chess?" Hustle asked, sitting in front of a chess board.

"A little. I only played a few times," Tae stated, seeing Hustle smile as he set the board up for them to play.

They played an intense game of chess and in less than three minutes Tae won and Hustle was amazed because the only person who could beat him was the person who taught him chess.

"Good game. You know a lot. You could have fooled me," Hustle said, taking a sip of the drink.

"I heard that a few times." Tae laughed hard.

"I heard of you when you started dealing wit Will. When I heard that my baby girl was dealing with you, I was upset. I had my goons watching you," Hustle told him.

"Smart."

"Yes, because I ain't know your intentions with my baby. I'm overprotective of her. Since Will killed my brother out of jealousy and envy, I could only think the rest of his bloodline was the same, but you're different. I have been watching you and another kid from Durham named Scrilla. He's Will's nephew, too," Hustle said.

Tae remembered hearing he had family in Durham, but he never really met that side of the family.

"I don't know him."

"I'm sure you don't, but I like the way you move. I want you to come work for me. I will make you a rich man, Tae. It's on you."

"Under one condition."

"What's that?"

"My crew is loyal and they with me every step of the way," Tae stated.

"Justin, huh? I know his mom. He's a loyal kid."

"Yeah." Tae was a little surprised at how much Hustle really knew.

"Ok deal, but I'ma tell you this up front: Never cross me and I won't double cross you. Also, never play with my money, or family or you will regret it." Hustle put on a fake smile.

"We family now. If I play you, I will play myself."

"True. Now let's go over a business plan," Hustle said.

***

Atlanta, GA

Justin flew out to Atlanta to fuck with Olivia. They had spent two days in a fancy hotel making love and having a ball.

They really cared for each other in a short period of time, but the only issue was Justin lived in North Carolina and Olivia lived in Atlanta.

He had to get back to Raleigh because Tae said he needed to speak to him ASAP. He hoped nobody got killed.

***

Spellman University, GA

Tajara had been stressing about her financial issues. She was late on her car note and phone bill. In a matter of days, her cellphone would be disconnected, and her car could be repossessed any day now.

She called Bri just to speak to her and see how she was doing. Tajara hadn't heard from her brother or sister in weeks.

"Bri."

"Tajara, how you been? Damn. You don't even call a bitch no more, funny hoe," Bri said on the phone.

"Girl, sorry. I been stressed about bills and all this school shit drove me crazy," Tajara said, getting out of her bed in her nightgown to fix some coffee.

"Bill?"

"Yeah, I'm behind."

"I'ma CashApp you 10,000. Just send me the info," Bri told her.

"10,000? You don't got that type of money."

"Just send the info, bitch. I'm coming down there soon. My boyfriend's from Atlanta, so I'ma visit some of his family," Bri said.

"Ok, stop by." Tajara talked for an hour, and she texted Bri her CashApp and the 10,000 popped up in seconds. She was overwhelmed.

Romell Tukes

Chapter 49
North Raleigh, N.C.

Big Zone's family was throwing a big cookout in Pullen Park. Lots of people came out to enjoy the hot summer day and have a good time today.

Big Zone had one of the biggest families in Raleigh. He and his crew were at a picnic table, eating and drinking while playing a game of spades with big money on the line.

"Uncle Ju, you just cut diamonds. How the fuck you leading with diamonds now?" Big Zone called his uncle out on his cheating.

"Huh, nephew? You tripping. I cut hearts," Uncle Ju said, looking around to see if anybody else was catching on to his old school game.

"Flip the last deck of cards over. You just closed," Roy said, who was Big Zone's cousin playing on his team.

"When everybody saw his hesitation, Big Zone snatched the deck of cards to see that he was right and his uncle was cheating.

"Nigga, you cheating old bastard," Big Zone said.

"Oh, man. I need my glasses, nephew. I thought that was a diamond. You know I'm still high from that good weed smoke," Uncle Ju told everybody before they all threw their hands up, finishing the game.

Big Zone had been going off, but he was not in the mood for dumb shit. Tomorrow he was flying out to the West Coast for a few weeks because there had been so much gun violence in the city. He knew he had to get low. Tae and his crew were slowly destroying everything he built, and he was losing family members.

Growing up, family was everything to him. He knew his lifestyle could affect those important to him.

"Big Zone, I got a call from niggas on German Street. They just got robbed and shot up," Big Zone's little homie Meek stated, hanging up his phone.

"Fuck! We gotta go!" Big Zone got up and five niggas followed him on his heels. Two trucks made their way to the entrance until three cars cut them off, slamming on the brakes.

Big Zone had his boy beep the horn, not knowing what was going on.

Four gunmen in ski masks with choppers started spraying up both trucks.

Tat, Tat, Tat, Tat, Tat, Tat, Tat, Tat …

Both of the SUVs were riddled with bullets, killing Big Zone and four more of his men. One of them survived with only a shot to the shoulder.

***

North Raleigh Apartments, N.C.

Tae and his team hopped out of the cars they just used to slide on Big Zone with and rushed into one of the buildings. The drivers of the cars were taking the hot cars to a local chop shop.

Inside, Justin told everybody to place the choppers in one bag. He would get rid of the guns.

"Now we all gotta hope Big Zone's dead. If not, we coming back ten times harder, but I think he done. Justin, call the guys to see if they robbed Zone's stash house on German Street," Tae stated.

"Got you, bruh." Justine went to the back of the room to make the call.

"Now that Big Zone's out the picture, we finna take over all his blocks and projects. I want y'all to spread the word that his blocks is our blocks now. Iight," Tae said, walking out of the crib.

Hustle asked Tae to do him a favor and kill Big Zone. Tae told Hustle he had been trying to for months with no luck. Hustle gave him Big Zone's location today and his stash house info. That's when Tae came up with his own plan to catch him slipping, and he did well.

Tae knew it was time to get to a real bag, especially with a steady plug like Hustle. The top was looking closer than he thought.

One of Tae cousins told him about a big family reunion in Durham on his dad's side. He planned to attend the reunion because he had never been around that side of the family.

In a few days, he planned to go, but he didn't even know his real dad. He knew it would feel weird, but he knew he could find some answers that his mom would never tell him.

***

Wake County, N.C.

Will had his windshield wipers going at a fast pace on his Range Rover as rain poured down on the SUV. He looked for Agent Folker's house, but the rain made it hard for him to see, plus it was dark outside.

"Here we go," Will said, turning off his headlights and cruising into the narrow driveway.

Will needed questions and since he had been hearing Agent Folker was asking about him and trying to build a case, he needed to see what he knew.

Some funny shit was going on and Will couldn't make sense of it. Bank and Spin both got ghost on him, it seemed like they just disappeared. Tae was his biggest fear now. Big Zone was found killed in a truck full of goons in Raleigh. He knew he fucked up by trying to get him killed too quick. Will had not heard from Spin since the Tae mission he sent him on, and he failed.

Will banged on the door getting soaked in rain.

"Who's there?" Agent Folker yelled on the other side of the door.

"Me ..." Will pulled out his gun, when he heard a lot of locks unlock.

The door opened, and he kicked it in rushing the agent with his gun, realizing the agent was butt ass naked.

"Please ..." Agent Folker was embarrassed his little stiff prick was out.

"Shut up and listen. I need to know -" Will was interrupted by two little kids running out of the living room naked. It was a boy and girl. He saw blood on the little girl's private and looked back at Agent Folker. He pistol-whipped him until he could not breathe or talk.

Will killed the agent, blacking out, forgetting about what he even came for. The little kids ran to the basement door and went downstairs.

Will cursed himself for not handling his task first, but seeing the little kids made him wild out because he hated rapists and creepy niggas.

Not knowing where to start, he searched the crib for files, but he searched the whole crib and took everything he could carry. One file caught his attention, and that was a photo of Bank that read Special Agent McQueen.

Will couldn't believe what he was looking at out of all people, Bank being an agent hurt his heart. He did more crimes wit Bank than anybody. Not to mention, he saw Bank kill more niggas than anybody in his crew. This was shocking news to him.

He went downstairs in the basement to see a dozen little kids trying to get out of the cages. It looked like a daycare jail. He couldn't believe it. All that went through his mind was how sick people could be.

Will freed all the kids and told them to call 411 and ask for child care services before he ran out with files.

Chapter 50
West Raleigh, N.C.

Rog loved Kingwood Projects on the West Side of the city. He was home from prison. He only had one objective, and that was to regain control over his hood.

Since his brother Glass was killed, he knew his hood was dry and dead, but he was bringing it back to life.

Fresh home, Rog found a new plug. He was ready to get some money. Hearing the news of Big Zone's death shocked him because he was in the city getting money for years.

When Rog was in jail, he couldn't stop hearing about a crew of young niggas from North Raleigh getting their names up. Rog recently heard those same young niggas were the ones who killed his brother Glass a few months back and Big Zone.

Posted up in his hood, he looked around as he used to daydream for ten years being in the feds.

Rog went to prison for shooting a man in broad daylight over a few dollars, but when Rog got caught, he had two bricks of pure coke on him.

Coming back to the same hood he grew up in and caught his case made him feel like Kingwood belonged to him, and he planned to take over.

First on his list was to flood his hood with drugs, then find out who this Tae and Justin kid were who he had been hearing about.

With three kids by three different baby mamas he had to get to a bag because child support wasn't gonna handle itself.

Rog joined his soldiers on the block as they all talked about dope boy dreams driving in luxury cars. What they didn't know was, Rog had something lined up for all of his guys in a day or so. He was gonna make sure his people ate good and locked down the West Side no matter what.

***

Raleigh, N.C.

Rena was all healed up and back to her regular self, and everything was going good besides going back to work.

She missed her job, but she quit and started looking for work elsewhere because her dad and Tae knew her safety would be in a lot of danger if she went back to the same place she almost got kidnapped.

"Hurry up!" Tae shouted to Rena, who stopped at an ATM outside of a bank to get some quick cash because Tae left his money behind.

"Boy, hush up!" Rena yelled back, waiting on 1500 to come out.

Rena was looking good today in an all white Louis Vuitton outfit with heels on.

They were on their way to his family reunion in Durham, and Rena tagged along on his arm like the trophy she was.

"You not finna get on my nerves today. Believe that." Rena pulled up in her new Audi knowing Tae could be very annoying and impatient.

"Sorry, I just like to be on time," Tae told her.

"We are, but I'm glad we got to spend some time together because you been leaving me stuck in that house forever," she stated, driving through the streets on her way to the nearest highway.

"Sorry," Tae said.

"It's been a lot of sorry's today. Are you sick or something? Let me feel your head," she said.

"Girl, stop playing. I just know when I'm wrong, so I have to take blame, feel me?" Tae told her, while texting Justin to tell him he would be out of town for a few hours at his family reunion.

"What happened with you and my dad? Y'all been chilling a lot lately?" She was being nosy.

"Why you so nosy?" He laughed.

"It's my dad, dummy," she replied.

"We good on business and shit."

"What business?"

"None of your business," Tae said, turning up the music on her, seeing her shaking her head.

***

Durham, N.C.

Scrilla came out to the family reunion in the park called Gator Max. It was a very big park with a lot of things to do from cookouts to swimming to basketball, football, handball, camping and having family events.

Scrilla and Main came out by themselves. They left their goons at home on the block, knowing 700 niggas didn't know how to act.

"This shit jumping, bro," Main said, hopping out of the car, seeing hundreds of people scattered all around the park.

"I got a big family. I guess because this shit litty," Scrilla said, seeing groups of bad bitches. Scrilla knew there was a big chance that most of the women he was looking at with phat asses were possibly related to him.

"Damn her ass phat, cuz." Main's eyes bulked as he walked by a chick whose ass was unbelievable.

"Chill, Dawg."

"Nigga, if that was my cousin, you would of bagged her," Main stated.

"True."

"Now she bad?" Main looked near the food bar.

"Who?"

"Shawty in the white," Main said, walking up towards the woman.

"Damn she is fire, but leave her alone, bru," Scrilla tried to tell Main, but it was too late. He was on her.

"Hey, sweetheart. I'm Main." He saw the woman look back and didn't say a word, but she tried to walk off as he continued to shoot his shot.

"You good, baby?" Tae walked up, seeing a dude trying to harass his girl.

"Yes. I was about to tell him I'm taken, but it's cool," Rena said with two plates of food. One for her and the other for Tae.

"My bad. I didn't know she was with you, cuz. My bad," Main said as Scrilla pulled up, hoping Main ain't start no shit.

"It's straight, bruh," Tae said.

"You from around here?" Scrilla asked, looking at Tae's jewelry and swag, knowing he was getting money somewhere.

"Raleigh," Tae said.

"Iight. I got some family out there," Scrilla said.

"Oh, Iight. I got some family out here, too," Tae shot back.

"Who dey be?" Main asked, knowing everybody.

"Scrilla," Tae said, seeing both men look at each other.

"I'm Scrilla, bruh. Who you?" Scrilla was a little surprised the man knew his name, but when it hit him, he had family in Raleigh, and it could have been him.

"I'm Tae. My cousin Low Dee was telling me about you and my Uncle Will," Tae said.

"I know who you are. We cousins. Will told me about you also," Scrilla said as Rena and Main just stood there watching the long lost family members chop it up.

After running into a few family members, Tae and Scrilla linked back up and chopped it up alone, drinking Henny.

"It's good to meet you but not to seem nosy, what type of shit you into down there in Raleigh?" Scrilla asked.

"I should be asking you the same thing," Tae shot back.

"I'm trying to get to a bag," Scrilla said.

"I'm on the same type of time."

"I was fucking with Will until he did some snake shit." Scrilla took a sip of Henny and pulled out a blunt.

"He got you too, huh?"

"You have no clue."

"Shit, that bitch nigga sent niggas to kill me," Tae said, seeing Scrilla's facial expression.

"Damn. You wanna know some crazy shit, bro? There is a nigga named Bank that be with him," Scrilla said.

"I know, bru."

"He told me he was a fed trying to build a case on Will." Scrilla shook his head.

"Oh shit, dawg. Ain't no way bruh moving that way." Tae couldn't believe it.

"Dude tried to get me to snitch to save myself, but I ain't finna go out like that. I can tell ole buddy had a different agenda in mind," Scrilla said.

"It'll be crazy if we came together and locked shit down in the city from Durham to Raleigh," Tae stated.

"The only issue with that is we need a plug. Will was my only source, but I can rob a few niggas," Scrilla stated seriously.

"Nah, cuz. No need for that, I got a plug," Tae said.

"He solid."

"Shit as real as it gets, bruh," Tae said thinking Hustle was the best thing that ever happened to him.

"'Iight. I'm with you, dawg, but first I want to clean up a little mess I got out here," Scrilla stated.

"You need help?"

"Nah, I got 700 Block. I'm a GD and my bro Main's a Crip. We got the city on lock." Scrilla looked around seeing his family listening to music chilling, dancing, playing games, and coming together. Even though neither one of them knew half of the people there, it was still good to see people enjoy themselves.

"I gotta head back to the city, but take my number, cuz. We can keep in touch," Tae told Scrilla.

"We family but family is nothing without real loyalty. That's all I ask from you." Scrilla needed to know that they were on the same page before opening the door. He learned from Will that just because a nigga is family don't make him blood or loyal.

"You got my loyalty if I got yours," Tae said. "Also, we should call ourselves Coke Boyz," Tae added.

"Fair, bruh. We locked in. Now let's get this paper," Scrilla said, giving his cousin and new business partner a hug. "Coke Boyz sounds good," Scrilla added.

"Facts." Tae knew this was the beginning to a new journey.

Tae and Scrilla went on about their way, and it was getting late, so Tae looked around for Rena. It didn't take long to find her sexy ass standing in the parking lot in all white.

He saw her talking to a dude in a black Rolls-Royce Wraith, but by the time Tae got closer the car pulled off.

"Who the fuck was you just talking to?" Tae asked Rena, knowing she wasn't the type to do shit behind his back.

"I don't know, but he told me to give you this." Rena handed him an envelope.

"Me?"

"Yeah and he looks just like you Tae, but he had Atlanta license plates on that nice ass car," Rena stated, seeing the people she was talking to earlier wave at her.

Tae did not waste any time opening the envelope to see what it was. He saw a plane ticket to Atlanta, GA, and a letter. Tae began to read the letter.

Hey Tae, my name is David. I know this may come as a surprise to you, but I'm your dad. I haven't seen you or your sisters in a long time, but I have my reasons. Just give me a chance to explain, but I still take responsibility for my wrongful acts as a man. I was a kid then. If you're willing to come sit and talk with me, it will be worth it. My address is at the bottom and number. I hope to hear from you soon. I knew you would be at the family reunion. I been coming up for years, hoping to see you so I can introduce myself and make up for lost time. I'm sorry, but I hope you can forgive me and understand my position. Sincerely,

Your father ...

Rena saw Tae's expression the whole time he read the letter, and she knew something was terribly wrong.

"You good?" she asked.

"Yeah."

"Who was that?" she really wanted to know.

"Nobody."

"Nobody I just -" Rena was cut off by Tae.

"Get in the car. We leaving." Tae got in the passenger seat and tossed the letter on the back seat.

She wanted to curse his ass out so bad, but she held it in and clutched her teeth.

They drove back to Raleigh, and Tae went to link up with Justin to tell him about everything that just took place.

***

East Durham, N.C.

M.I. had been calling YN all day, so he could pick up his work M.I. had for him before he slid off to New York for a little while.

YN drove his new Porsche with the large frog eyes to his location, where M.I. was awaiting him.

His gang 600 Block just was snatched up by the feds, only ten of them, so YN had been under the radar and watching his back.

The 700 Block niggas had been getting deep and trying to slowly but surely force their way throughout the city. The last shoot out, he had YN lost his unborn seed and girlfriend. That hurt him. What he couldn't figure out was how Scrilla knew Stacy. He was confused about that, but he left it alone because it was a dead issue now.

Pulling into the YMCA parking lot, he saw M.I. leaning on the hood of his car smoking a cigarette, looking frustrated.

"What the fuck, YN this shit ain't legal my nigga," M.I. said seeing YN get out of his new SUV.

"My bad. Shit been a little crazy," YN told him.

"One of the spots was robbed the other day. I think it was them 700 Block niggas. You need to take care of them," M.I. demanded.

"I just told you shit been all bad. Ten of my men got picked up by the boys a few days ago."

"Boyz? What boys?" M.I. asked.

"Nigga, them feds."

"Shit, I know it." M.I. started tripping, going in panic mode because he knew someone was watching him.

"You good?"

"How you know, little nigga," M.I. snapped on him.

"Because I ain't get hit," YN told him

"Look, get this shit out of my trunk, and I'm going out of state," M.I. said, rushing to get the drugs out of his trunk that he had for YN.

M.I. went to get the 17 keys of dope and five keys of coke he had left.

When M.I. grabbed the bag, he felt cold steel to the back of his head as YN snatched the duffle bag out of his hand.

"Raise up, fool," YN said, seeing how scared M.I. was, but also shocked to see YN out of all people line him up.

"You snake nigga," M.I. said.

"I robbed your spot the other day. How you think I got that Porsche, dumb ass nigga?" YN told him with the gun between M.I.'s eyes now.

"This is what it comes down to, huh? Greed bro?" M.I. said.

"Hell yeah, bitch nigga. Now I gotta go. Time is money," YN stated before pulling the trigger on the FN handgun blowing M.I.'s face off, which was a nasty sight.

YN got in his car and gave himself a positive self-talk about his good deed. Now YN could put his next plan together which was to find a new plug then rebuild his crew because he had been losing men and taking a lot of losses. YN had enough keys to hold him over until he found a plug.

It took a few minutes for him to get to his stash house. YN parked across the street and jumped out with the duffle bag, feeling himself thinking about getting rid of the FN gun.

"YN, that was smooth," a voice said, appearing from the shadows. YN pulled out his gun.

"Now, now, play nice. If I was you, I wouldn't do that." Spin came out of the bushes.

"Who the hell are you?" YN asked, ready to shoot.

"I'm da nigga who gonna help you take over the city and eliminate Scrilla and Will together. We can turn this shit upside down," Spin said, seeing he was catching YN attention now.

"Come inside. Let's talk," YN told him, leading the way, feeling that this was worth his while ...

To Be Continued...
Coke Boys 2
Coming Soon

Lock Down Publications and Ca$h Presents assisted publishing packages.

BASIC PACKAGE $499
Editing
Cover Design
Formatting

UPGRADED PACKAGE $800
Typing
Editing
Cover Design
Formatting

ADVANCE PACKAGE $1,200
Typing
Editing
Cover Design
Formatting
Copyright registration
Proofreading
Upload book to Amazon

LDP SUPREME PACKAGE $1,500
Typing
Editing
Cover Design
Formatting
Copyright registration
Proofreading
Set up Amazon account
Upload book to Amazon
Advertise on LDP Amazon and Facebook page

***Other services available upon request. Additional charges may apply

Lock Down Publications
P.O. Box 944
Stockbridge, GA 30281-9998
Phone # 470 303-9761

Submission Guideline

Submit the first three chapters of your completed manuscript to ldpsubmissions@gmail.com, subject line: Your book's title. The manuscript must be in a .doc file and sent as an attachment. Document should be in Times New Roman, double spaced and in size 12 font. Also, provide your synopsis and full contact information. If sending multiple submissions, they must each be in a separate email.

Have a story but no way to send it electronically? You can still submit to LDP/Ca$h Presents. Send in the first three chapters, written or typed, of your completed manuscript to:

LDP: Submissions Dept
Po Box 944
Stockbridge, Ga 30281

DO NOT send original manuscript. Must be a duplicate.

Provide your synopsis and a cover letter containing your full contact information.

Thanks for considering LDP and Ca$h Presents.

NEW RELEASES

QUEEN OF THE ZOO 2 by BLACK MIGO
THE HEART OF A SAVAGE 4 by JIBRIL
WILLIAMS
THE BIRTH OF A GANGSTER 2 by DELMONT
PLAYER
LOYAL TO THE SOIL 3 by JIBRIL WILLIAMS
COKE BOYS by ROMELL TUKES

Coke Boys

STRAIGHT BEAST MODE III

De'Kari

KINGPIN KILLAZ IV

STREET KINGS III

PAID IN BLOOD III

CARTEL KILLAZ IV

DOPE GODS III

Hood Rich

SINS OF A HUSTLA II

ASAD

RICH $AVAGE II

By Martell Troublesome Bolden

YAYO V

Bred In The Game 2

S. Allen

CREAM III

THE STREETS WILL TALK II

By Yolanda Moore

SON OF A DOPE FIEND III

HEAVEN GOT A GHETTO II

By Renta

LOYALTY AIN'T PROMISED III

By Keith Williams

I'M NOTHING WITHOUT HIS LOVE II

SINS OF A THUG II

TO THE THUG I LOVED BEFORE II

IN A HUSTLER I TRUST II

By Monet Dragun

QUIET MONEY IV

EXTENDED CLIP III

Romell Tukes

THUG LIFE IV

By **Trai'Quan**

THE STREETS MADE ME IV

By **Larry D. Wright**

IF YOU CROSS ME ONCE II

ANGEL IV

By **Anthony Fields**

THE STREETS WILL NEVER CLOSE IV

By **K'ajji**

HARD AND RUTHLESS III

KILLA KOUNTY III

By **Khufu**

MONEY GAME III

By **Smoove Dolla**

JACK BOYS VS DOPE BOYS II

A GANGSTA'S QUR'AN V

COKE GIRLZ II

COKE BOYS II

By **Romell Tukes**

MURDA WAS THE CASE II

Elijah R. Freeman

THE STREETS NEVER LET GO II

By **Robert Baptiste**

AN UNFORESEEN LOVE III

By **Meesha**

KING OF THE TRENCHES III

by **GHOST & TRANAY ADAMS**

MONEY MAFIA II

By **Jibril Williams**

QUEEN OF THE ZOO III

Coke Boys

By **Black Migo**
VICIOUS LOYALTY III

By Kingpen
A GANGSTA'S PAIN III

By J-Blunt
CONFESSIONS OF A JACKBOY III

By Nicholas Lock
GRIMEY WAYS II

By Ray Vinci
KING KILLA II

By Vincent "Vitto" Holloway
BETRAYAL OF A THUG II

By Fre$h
THE MURDER QUEENS II

By Michael Gallon
THE BIRTH OF A GANGSTER III

By Delmont Player
TREAL LOVE II

By Le'Monica Jackson
FOR THE LOVE OF BLOOD II

By Jamel Mitchell
RAN OFF ON DA PLUG II

By Paper Boi Rari
HOOD CONSIGLIERE II

By Keese
PRETTY GIRLS DO NASTY THINGS II

By Nicole Goosby
PROTÉGÉ OF A LEGEND II

By Corey Robinson
IT'S JUST ME AND YOU II

Romell Tukes

By Ah'Million

Available Now

RESTRAINING ORDER **I & II**
By **CA$H & Coffee**
LOVE KNOWS NO BOUNDARIES **I II & III**
By **Coffee**
RAISED AS A GOON I, II, III & IV
BRED BY THE SLUMS I, II, III
BLAST FOR ME I & II
ROTTEN TO THE CORE I II III
A BRONX TALE I, II, III
DUFFLE BAG CARTEL I II III IV V VI
HEARTLESS GOON I II III IV V
A SAVAGE DOPEBOY I II
DRUG LORDS I II III
CUTTHROAT MAFIA I II
KING OF THE TRENCHES
By **Ghost**
LAY IT DOWN **I & II**
LAST OF A DYING BREED I II
BLOOD STAINS OF A SHOTTA I & II III
By **Jamaica**
LOYAL TO THE GAME I II III
LIFE OF SIN I, II III
By **TJ & Jelissa**

Coke Boys

Romell Tukes

PUSH IT TO THE LIMIT

By **Bre' Hayes**

BLOOD OF A BOSS **I, II, III, IV, V**

SHADOWS OF THE GAME

TRAP BASTARD

By **Askari**

THE STREETS BLEED MURDER **I, II & III**

THE HEART OF A GANGSTA I II& III

By **Jerry Jackson**

CUM FOR ME I II III IV V VI VII VIII

An **LDP Erotica Collaboration**

BRIDE OF A HUSTLA **I II & II**

THE FETTI GIRLS **I, II& III**

CORRUPTED BY A GANGSTA I, II III, IV

BLINDED BY HIS LOVE

THE PRICE YOU PAY FOR LOVE I, II ,III

DOPE GIRL MAGIC I II III

By **Destiny Skai**

WHEN A GOOD GIRL GOES BAD

By **Adrienne**

THE COST OF LOYALTY I II III

By Kweli

A GANGSTER'S REVENGE **I II III & IV**

THE BOSS MAN'S DAUGHTERS I II III IV V

A SAVAGE LOVE **I & II**

BAE BELONGS TO ME I II

A HUSTLER'S DECEIT I, II, III

WHAT BAD BITCHES DO I, II, III

SOUL OF A MONSTER I II III

KILL ZONE

Coke Boys

A DOPE BOY'S QUEEN I II III

TIL DEATH

By **Aryanna**

A KINGPIN'S AMBITON

A KINGPIN'S AMBITION **II**

I MURDER FOR THE DOUGH

By **Ambitious**

TRUE SAVAGE I II III IV V VI VII

DOPE BOY MAGIC I, II, III

MIDNIGHT CARTEL I II III

CITY OF KINGZ I II

NIGHTMARE ON SILENT AVE

THE PLUG OF LIL MEXICO II

CLASSIC CITY

By **Chris Green**

A DOPEBOY'S PRAYER

By **Eddie "Wolf" Lee**

THE KING CARTEL **I, II & III**

By **Frank Gresham**

THESE NIGGAS AIN'T LOYAL **I, II & III**

By **Nikki Tee**

GANGSTA SHYT **I II &III**

By **CATO**

THE ULTIMATE BETRAYAL

By **Phoenix**

BOSS'N UP **I , II & III**

By **Royal Nicole**

I LOVE YOU TO DEATH

By **Destiny J**

I RIDE FOR MY HITTA

I STILL RIDE FOR MY HITTA

By **Misty Holt**

LOVE & CHASIN' PAPER

By **Qay Crockett**

TO DIE IN VAIN

SINS OF A HUSTLA

By **ASAD**

BROOKLYN HUSTLAZ

By **Boogsy Morina**

BROOKLYN ON LOCK I & II

By **Sonovia**

GANGSTA CITY

By **Teddy Duke**

A DRUG KING AND HIS DIAMOND I & II III

A DOPEMAN'S RICHES

HER MAN, MINE'S TOO I, II

CASH MONEY HO'S

THE WIFEY I USED TO BE I II

PRETTY GIRLS DO NASTY THINGS

By Nicole Goosby

TRAPHOUSE KING **I II & III**

KINGPIN KILLAZ I II III

STREET KINGS I II

PAID IN BLOOD **I II**

CARTEL KILLAZ I II III

DOPE GODS I II

By **Hood Rich**

LIPSTICK KILLAH **I, II, III**

CRIME OF PASSION I II & III

FRIEND OR FOE I II III

Coke Boys

By **Mimi**
STEADY MOBBN' **I, II, III**
THE STREETS STAINED MY SOUL I II III
By **Marcellus Allen**
WHO SHOT YA **I, II, III**
SON OF A DOPE FIEND I II
HEAVEN GOT A GHETTO
Renta
GORILLAZ IN THE BAY **I II III IV**
TEARS OF A GANGSTA I II
3X KRAZY I II
STRAIGHT BEAST MODE I II
DE'KARI
TRIGGADALE I II III
MURDAROBER WAS THE CASE
Elijah R. Freeman
GOD BLESS THE TRAPPERS I, II, III
THESE SCANDALOUS STREETS I, II, III
FEAR MY GANGSTA I, II, III IV, V
THESE STREETS DON'T LOVE NOBODY I, II
BURY ME A G I, II, III, IV, V
A GANGSTA'S EMPIRE I, II, III, IV
THE DOPEMAN'S BODYGAURD I II
THE REALEST KILLAZ I II III
THE LAST OF THE OGS I II III
Tranay Adams
THE STREETS ARE CALLING
Duquie Wilson
MARRIED TO A BOSS I II III
By Destiny Skai & Chris Green

Romell Tukes

KINGZ OF THE GAME I II III IV V VI
Playa Ray
SLAUGHTER GANG I II III
RUTHLESS HEART I II III
By Willie Slaughter
FUK SHYT
By Blakk Diamond
DON'T F#CK WITH MY HEART I II
By Linnea
ADDICTED TO THE DRAMA I II III
IN THE ARM OF HIS BOSS II
By Jamila
YAYO I II III IV
A SHOOTER'S AMBITION I II
BRED IN THE GAME
By S. Allen
TRAP GOD I II III
RICH $AVAGE
MONEY IN THE GRAVE I II III
By Martell Troublesome Bolden
FOREVER GANGSTA
GLOCKS ON SATIN SHEETS I II
By Adrian Dulan
TOE TAGZ I II III IV
LEVELS TO THIS SHYT I II
IT'S JUST ME AND YOU
By Ah'Million
KINGPIN DREAMS I II III
RAN OFF ON DA PLUG
By Paper Boi Rari

Coke Boys

CONFESSIONS OF A GANGSTA I II III IV
CONFESSIONS OF A JACKBOY I II
By Nicholas Lock
I'M NOTHING WITHOUT HIS LOVE
SINS OF A THUG
TO THE THUG I LOVED BEFORE
A GANGSTA SAVED XMAS
IN A HUSTLER I TRUST
By Monet Dragun
CAUGHT UP IN THE LIFE I II III
THE STREETS NEVER LET GO
By Robert Baptiste
NEW TO THE GAME I II III
MONEY, MURDER & MEMORIES I II III
By **Malik D. Rice**
LIFE OF A SAVAGE I II III
A GANGSTA'S QUR'AN I II III IV
MURDA SEASON I II III
GANGLAND CARTEL I II III
CHI'RAQ GANGSTAS I II III
KILLERS ON ELM STREET I II III
JACK BOYZ N DA BRONX I II III
A DOPEBOY'S DREAM I II III
JACK BOYS VS DOPE BOYS
COKE GIRLZ
COKE BOYS
By Romell Tukes
LOYALTY AIN'T PROMISED I II
By Keith Williams
QUIET MONEY I II III

Romell Tukes

THUG LIFE I II III

EXTENDED CLIP I II

By **Trai'Quan**

THE STREETS MADE ME I II III

By **Larry D. Wright**

THE ULTIMATE SACRIFICE I, II, III, IV, V, VI

KHADIFI

IF YOU CROSS ME ONCE

ANGEL I II III

IN THE BLINK OF AN EYE

By **Anthony Fields**

THE LIFE OF A HOOD STAR

By Ca$h & Rashia Wilson

THE STREETS WILL NEVER CLOSE I II III

By K'ajji

CREAM I II

THE STREETS WILL TALK

By Yolanda Moore

NIGHTMARES OF A HUSTLA I II III

By King Dream

CONCRETE KILLA I II III

VICIOUS LOYALTY I II

By Kingpen

HARD AND RUTHLESS I II

MOB TOWN 251

THE BILLIONAIRE BENTLEYS I II III

By Von Diesel

GHOST MOB

Stilloan Robinson

MOB TIES I II III IV V VI

Coke Boys

By SayNoMore
BODYMORE MURDERLAND I II III
THE BIRTH OF A GANGSTER I II
By Delmont Player
FOR THE LOVE OF A BOSS
By C. D. Blue
MOBBED UP I II III IV
THE BRICK MAN I II III IV
THE COCAINE PRINCESS I II III IV V
By King Rio
KILLA KOUNTY I II III
By Khufu
MONEY GAME I II
By Smoove Dolla
A GANGSTA'S KARMA I II
By FLAME
KING OF THE TRENCHES I II
by **GHOST & TRANAY ADAMS**
QUEEN OF THE ZOO I II
By **Black Migo**
GRIMEY WAYS
By Ray Vinci
XMAS WITH AN ATL SHOOTER
By Ca$h & Destiny Skai
KING KILLA
By Vincent "Vitto" Holloway
BETRAYAL OF A THUG
By Fre$h
THE MURDER QUEENS
By Michael Gallon

TREAL LOVE
By Le'Monica Jackson
FOR THE LOVE OF BLOOD
By Jamel Mitchell
HOOD CONSIGLIERE
By Keese
PROTÉGÉ OF A LEGEND
By Corey Robinson

BOOKS BY LDP'S CEO, CA$H

TRUST IN NO MAN

TRUST IN NO MAN 2

TRUST IN NO MAN 3

BONDED BY BLOOD

SHORTY GOT A THUG

THUGS CRY

THUGS CRY 2

THUGS CRY 3

TRUST NO BITCH

TRUST NO BITCH 2

TRUST NO BITCH 3

TIL MY CASKET DROPS

RESTRAINING ORDER

RESTRAINING ORDER 2

IN LOVE WITH A CONVICT

LIFE OF A HOOD STAR

XMAS WITH AN ATL SHOOTER